CW01019891

REFUGE

JACKIE
FRENCH

REFUGE

Angus&Robertson
An imprint of HarperCollins*Children's Books*

Angus&Robertson
An imprint of HarperCollins*Children'sBooks*, Australia

First published in Australia in 2013
by HarperCollins*Publishers* Australia Pty Limited
ABN 36 009 913 517
harpercollins.com.au

Copyright © Jackie French and E French 2013

The right of Jackie French to be identified as the author of this work
has been asserted by her in accordance with the *Copyright Amendment
(Moral Rights) Act 2000*.

This work is copyright. Apart from any use as permitted under the
Copyright Act 1968, no part may be reproduced, copied, scanned, stored in a
retrieval system, recorded, or transmitted, in any form or by any means,
without the prior written permission of the publisher.

HarperCollins*Publishers*
Level 13, 201 Elizabeth Street, Sydney NSW 2000, Australia
Unit D1, 63 Apollo Drive, Rosedale, Auckland 0632, New Zealand
A 53, Sector 57, Noida, UP, India
77–85 Fulham Palace Road, London W6 8JB, United Kingdom
2 Bloor Street East, 20th floor, Toronto, Ontario M4W 1A8, Canada
195 Broadway, New York NY 10007, USA

National Library of Australia Cataloguing-in-Publication entry:

French, Jackie.
    Refuge / Jackie French.
    1st ed.
    ISBN: 978 0 7322 9617 9 (pbk.)
    For ages 10 and over.
    Refugee children—Juvenile fiction.
    Immigrant children—Juvenile fiction.
A823.3

Cover design by Jane Waterhouse, HarperCollins Design Studio
Cover image © Alain Keler/Sygma/Corbis
Author photograph by Kelly Sturgiss
Typeset in Bookman 10/14pt by Kirby Jones
Printed and bound in Australia by McPhersons Printing Group
The papers used by HarperCollins in the manufacture of this book
are a natural, recyclable product made from wood grown in sustainable
plantation forests. The fibre source and manufacturing processes meet
recognised international environmental standards, and carry certification.

To the Sisters of St Joseph, who in the 1960s made an Indigenous girl captain of the school debating team, when many schools found a pretext to exclude Indigenous children, most wouldn't even let girls debate at all, and even fewer would make a girl captain. (That team managed to win their first debate. After that they were unstoppable. They won the championship.) Those indomitable women gave hope and education to so many barefoot kids. This book is dedicated to them, with admiration and enormous gratitude for their strength and inspiration.

CHAPTER 1

Northwest of Australia

The sky was grey. The sea was grey too. It shivered. The sea filled the world. Its fingers slapped at the tiny boat with its grey timbers and grey metal framework at one end.

Australia was somewhere behind that line where sea met sky. It was hard to believe in the golden beaches of Australia, here in this universe of grey.

Even the other passengers were grey: weary faces, faded clothes. Faris had counted thirty-four on the deck, apart from himself and Jadda: men in trousers and kurtas; women in scarves or hijabs. Three children, younger than him, sat by their mothers as though they were used to waiting — as though waiting had been their entire lives.

Only Jadda was bareheaded, her grey hair held back with two clips. Jadda had flung away her hijab as the boat cast off from the ramshackle jetty in Indonesia.

For a while she and Faris had used the fabric as a thin cushion between them and the splintered deck of the boat. But as the wind rose, and the foam and spray spat in their faces, the hijab had grown sodden. Now it lay in a small wet clump, next to the one plastic bag the two men who crewed the boat had allowed them to bring. Everything else Faris owned was wrapped in more plastic bags hidden around his waist — his birth certificate and other papers that Jadda said were the most important things he owned.

There hadn't been much to leave behind. There had already been so many leavings in the past year, since the phone call that ripped the night, ripped his life. The 'friend' saying urgently that the police were coming to their flat, just as they had come for his father five years earlier. The sharp voice on the phone had said that Jadda must take him now, at once, to safety.

He'd had time to thrust two shirts, a pair of trousers, his mobile phone, two books and even his laptop into his schoolbag. He had clutched the bag to him as they huddled in the back of the truck driving them across the border.

They had sold his laptop in the first week at the refugee camp, for there was no electricity, at least not in the long rows of tents in which they lived.

But he kept the phone, tied around his waist in one of Jadda's old stockings, where the camp toughs wouldn't notice it, turning it on only once a week to save the battery, at the time his father called from Australia, his voice a stranger's now after five years away.

'I'm sorry,' his father had said on that first phone call to the camp. 'I am sorry that I have led you to this.'

Faris said nothing. He wanted to yell: 'What have you done? Why did you do this to us?'

He couldn't.

'Don't ask,' Jadda had told him, on that night five years back when his father had staggered home, blood on his jacket, his face like someone had smudged his eyes with black polish. His father had shaken his head when Faris tried to hug him, and vanished to talk to Jadda in the kitchen. Faris could hear their muttered voices.

Jadda had come out. 'Go to the pictures,' she said, pressing money into his hand. 'Now!'

Faris had never gone to the pictures at night. He had never gone to the pictures alone. He peered into the kitchen, where his father sat, with that white blank face.

When Faris got back, his father had gone. Blood stained the kitchen table.

Jadda's face was cold marble. 'Pack,' she said. 'We have to go.'

'Where? Why?'

What had happened? His father was an important man, a doctor at the hospital. Jadda had given him a gold-plated stethoscope to wear around his neck. His office had his framed certificates on the walls. Trouble came to other families. Not to men like his father!

'The police have taken your father. Don't ask more.'

'Why not?'

She looked at him steadily. 'You can't tell what you do not know. Trust me. It is safer if you can say truthfully, "No one told me anything." Now pack. Fast!'

Faris packed. Jadda made phone call after phone call. At last friends arrived to help them move what they could to a small flat over a carpet shop. Faris wondered if it would be harder for the police to find them there, to question them or torture them, to see if a rebel's family knew where other rebels might be.

How could his father be a rebel? Rebels shouted and drew slogans on the walls. Rebels plotted. They didn't live in houses with fine gardens, with rich carpets on the floor. Their sons didn't go to good schools.

He had not gone back to his good school. Jadda had not gone back to the academy where she had taught English literature and language. Had the schools asked them not to come, the son and mother of a rebel?

He didn't know. He didn't ask.

Jadda sold her jewellery, piece by piece, so they could live. She taught him his lessons at their tiny kitchen table. Friends avoided them, or perhaps they avoided friends.

They lived for three years, waiting for the police to drag them off for questioning, or even, like a miracle, for his father to come grinning through the door, in his good jacket, with the bloodstains gone. It had all been a mistake, he wasn't a rebel at all.

Neither happened.

And then the call from his father two years earlier. His father had been freed, perhaps to see if he would lead the police to real rebels. But he hadn't come to see his son and mother. He had hidden in a truck that took him over the border to a refugee camp.

But he was not in the camp now. He was in a place called Australia. He could call them each week. He was trying to save money, was trying to find a way for them to come to Australia too. He would call again.

Jadda cried that night, deep gulping sobs, when she thought Faris was asleep. But instead he sat with his laptop on his bed, looking at Australia.

It was beautiful. A rich country. Bright fish swam on its Great Barrier Reef. Tourists wandered on golden beaches. Its Opera House gleamed under the blue sky. Faris was glad his father was near an opera house, where he could hear the music that he loved.

His father phoned at the same time each week after that, talking mostly to Jadda, for a few minutes only. Phone calls were expensive. There was little jewellery left.

Every night Faris looked at the tourist sites for Australia. Big breakfasts of pineapple and melon. Infinity pools that rippled towards the sea. Beaches, beaches, beaches, where golden sand met blue sky and turquoise sea or forest.

And then the urgent call, not from his father: the one that sent him and Jadda into hiding. The police were coming for them, to force his father to return, to give them information. He and Jadda scurried through shadowed streets to a waiting car, hid under blankets in the back, trying not to look at those who helped them.

You could not tell what you didn't know.

The car took them to a warehouse. In the warehouse was a crate. They stepped into the crate. Faris heard the lid go down, heard a truck's engine, felt the bump as the crate was loaded on it.

The drive seemed short. It also seemed to take longer than his whole life so far.

The truck stopped. The back opened. The lid was lifted off the box. They struggled, stiff, around other boxes, filled with things, not people. Faris helped Jadda down.

The road stretched to nothing on either side.

The driver pointed. 'The refugee camp is that way. I do not know you,' he added. 'If you see me, do not nod or smile. Go with God.'

He drove away.

They walked. They found tents, barbed wire, dust. Food was given out from trucks each day. They lined up to fill a bottle at the camp's only tap.

People waited.

Jadda didn't wait.

Jadda sold a gold bracelet in the refugee camp to a guard, to get them in the Jeep to the small airport. Her mother's ruby earrings bought tickets on a plane to a larger airport, and the flight to Indonesia, and the tiny room there in which they lived, where the air tasted of bad soup. Strange bugs crawled over him while he slept and others buzzed around his head when it was light.

They did not go to the International Organisation for Refugees Camp. 'You wait four years, or five there, before you can go to Australia,' said Jadda. 'You must go to school, to university, not spend your life here waiting.' She wouldn't let him learn Bahasa, to go to the local school. He must speak English, for Australia.

Jadda's ruby ring paid for their passage on the boat. There was no more jewellery now. The man at the jetty had even taken his precious mobile phone.

Now there was just the boat, the passengers, the sky, the sea.

'Jadda?'

Jadda sat with her arms around her knees, her hair the colour of the rain. 'What is it?' She spoke in English. They had spoken English together ever since his father reached Australia, ever since they had begun to dream they might join him there.

He wanted to say, 'I'm scared.' Not just of the ocean, but what was ahead of them. There was nowhere to run to, after Australia. Somehow that was more frightening than the dangers of the sea. But a boy of thirteen couldn't say that to his grandmother. It would be cowardly to say he was scared at all.

Somehow Jadda understood. She smiled. The grey figure beside him turned back into the Jadda he had known. 'Look,' she said softly. She pointed to the shiver where grey sea met the great sky. 'Australia is over there. Shut your eyes, Faris.'

When he was small and scared of night monsters, Jadda had told him to shut his eyes, to dream of a gold light about his bed.

'What should I dream of, Jadda?'

'Australia. A wonderful Australia. A home,' she said softly.

'It … it doesn't seem possible.'

'You must believe that everything is possible.'

'But some things aren't possible! It's not possible to fly like a bird, or … or to jump across an ocean.' If only he could jump across this grey sea, onto Australia.

'Impossible is a word for people who don't want to try,' said Jadda fiercely. 'If the people who invented aeroplanes thought "impossible", then we'd never have soared to the clouds. If enough people say "impossible", then no one will try to fight evil, to make the world good. How can you reach your dreams if you don't imagine them?'

Faris shut his eyes. The grey world vanished. The sky was blue, the beach was gold, the rocks were red, the fish swam in bright colours through the coral of the reef.

In Australia he would go to a school like the ones he had seen on the internet. He could picture it: a big green lawn and a red-brick building with green plants growing on the walls; and laughing children sitting on the grass with their laptops and friends.

He felt himself begin to smile.

'What can you see?' whispered Jadda.

'Our house.' A house for him, and Jadda and his father, a big house just as the family of a doctor should have. A wardrobe filled with new jeans and T-shirts, instead of a spare shirt and a change of underwear in a plastic bag.

'What is it like?'

'It's two storeys high.' He tried to think what Jadda would like too. 'There are walls with bookcases up

to the ceiling. Every book Jane Austen ever wrote.'
He heard Jadda laugh softly at that. Jadda loved the
English writer Jane Austen, with her far-off world of
women dancing in bonnets. 'You have a pet koala.'

'What's its name?'

Faris found himself grinning. How long had it
been since he'd grinned? He opened his eyes. 'It's *your*
koala. You have to name him.'

'Nosey,' said Jadda. 'Because of his short nose.'

Something was wrong. He felt his grin slide from his
face as he looked around. The two crewmen huddled
over the engine, their voices sharp as the wind grew in
strength. Faris was good at languages, but theirs was
one he didn't know.

The sky had grown a darker grey. The ocean was
black.

Faris looked at the people next to him: a man with
his arms around a woman and a girl, three perhaps,
another in the woman's arms. He wondered if they
spoke English.

He tried to imagine them in Australian clothes, the
sort he had seen on the internet. They would wear jeans,
the man a flowered shirt perhaps as he walked along
the golden beach, the children playing in the waves.

The waves smashed at the sides of the boat. Faris
shut his eyes and tried to see the beach again. He had
never seen a real golden beach, only the rickety jetty
that poked out of grey mud.

Thunder growled, not just above, but all around.

He and Jadda would live near the beach. All
Australians lived near the beach, except those who

were Aboriginal and had black skins and lived near a huge red rock called Uluru.

The boat lurched again. The storm slapped them, sweeping through the grey. Faris looked up as one of the crew thrust an old tin can into his hand. The crewman gestured to the water in the boat. The meaning was clear. Faris began to bail out the water, can by can. Around them others were doing the same, with cans and hands, a bucket.

The rain hit so hard it stung. Foam flew through the air, dripping like shaving cream. The boat rose up, then crashed back down. Wet wave tops slashed their faces. A child screamed. Faris heard the words of prayers, a woman's sobs.

Not Jadda's. She moved closer, her arms around him now.

He lifted his voice above the wind. 'Is the boat going to turn back?' Indonesia was closer to them than Australia. He wasn't sure what he was scared of most: the storm or not reaching that land beyond the line of sea and sky.

Jadda shook her head. She spoke close to his ear, so others wouldn't hear. 'The owner of this boat makes too much money from each trip to turn back now.'

'But if … if the boat sinks, he won't have a boat.'

'I don't think the boat is worth much,' said Jadda. She hesitated, then added, 'I think the boats are chosen so it doesn't matter if they sink.'

'And the people on it? His crew?'

'I don't think he values them either. Our money is

only released to him when we land in Australia. If we turn back, he gets nothing.'

Faris glanced at the crew as he scooped out water again. One man was still bent over the engine, the other bailing. Faris had thought this was a fishing boat, that the owner would be on it. Instead the owner might be a rich man, far away.

Scoop and throw, scoop and throw ...

A wave slapped his face. He snorted to get the water out of his nose.

He looked at the other passengers, the children huddled with their mothers, the men and some of the women bailing. Jadda had paid fourteen thousand American dollars so that the two of them could step into this grey boat.

The boat twisted so sharply he had to clutch the railing. On the other side of the boat a father clutched his child. Scoop and throw, scoop and throw ...

How had the other people in this boat found so much money? Were some of them rich, or did they have rich families? Were all of them desperate, like him and Jadda? Were some of them criminals, trying to sneak into Australia?

The boat lunged again. A wave rose high above them. For seven long seconds it seemed that it would crash on top of them. Somehow the boat managed to find its way up and along it, plunging down the other side.

Scoop and throw, scoop and throw. His arms ached. His throat was salty and bitter. A woman sobbed down the other end of the boat.

Faris tried to multiply seven thousand dollars by the number of people on the boat, to keep his mind away from the lurch and crash. But all his mind could hold were waves and water.

The boat would sink. The storm would break it into twigs and rust. The passengers would slide down, down, down, into the grey water. Were the depths of the ocean storm-tossed too? Or would the water feel calm as it sucked his life ...

Jadda moved closer. 'Faris?'

He nodded, trying not to show his fear. 'Will the boat break up?'

She looked at him, her gaze clear. Jadda never lied. That was why you couldn't ask her questions when the answers were too hard. 'Perhaps. But if it does ...' He didn't want to hear the words. This boat was all the safety in his world. But her voice was steady in his ear. 'Grab hold of anything that floats. A piece of wood. Anything to keep your head above the water. A rescue ship will come,' she hesitated and added, 'perhaps.'

She took a harsh, deep breath. 'Faris, will you promise me something? Please, will you promise?'

'Promise what?'

She spoke close to his ear again, so he could hear. 'Promise that you will try to live. No matter what. Don't think of me. Think of your new life. Think of Australia. Never forget the Australia of your dreams. To get there you have to live! Please, promise.'

'I won't forget. I will think of Australia.' A wave reared up. They froze as somehow the boat shuddered up and past.

Jadda reached into their bag and brought out the flask of water. She held it to him. 'Drink it. Drink it all.'

We should save some for later, he thought. And then, Perhaps there won't be a later. That is why I need to drink it now. For strength, to keep going, to get to Australia.

He said, 'You drink half. Then me.'

He thought she was going to refuse. But he was too old now to do his grandmother's bidding just because she said so. Instead she took a sip, then another. He knew that was all she'd take.

He took the flask and drank the rest. If fresh water could make him stronger, he could help Jadda.

He put the flask in their plastic bag. He bailed again.

Scoop and throw, scoop and throw. A man vomited. The storm carried the muck away.

Waves. Wind. Air thick with water for so long that at last even the screams and sobbing stopped.

Faris tried to keep his eyes on the tin can as he scooped the water up and out. *Think of Australia*, whispered Jadda's voice in his mind. *Don't think of the storm, the fragile rusty boat.* He tried to think of a quiet bedroom, with clean sheets. But how could any dream help you survive when the world was ripped by storm?

The small grey boat still floated. And slowly the waves began to slacken.

At last Faris looked up. The sky was pale again, as though the darkness had fallen with the rain. A sea like a rocky plain. He turned to Jadda, to try to smile at her, to tell her that dreaming of good things worked.

He had ridden the storm without screaming. They had survived.

And then he saw the wave.

Had it waited till the storm had eased, the better to show its majesty? It reared like a sea beast from the ocean depths, as high as a three-storey building. Foam danced about the top.

Jadda's hand gripped his. She yelled, 'I love you!'

The wave crashed down.

Pain. His body was crushed down, then up, then sideways, and down again. The water tried to tear him apart. Water that was green, not grey, and filled with bubbles. A sensation that was only down, down, down, but no knowledge of where 'up' might be. His arms and legs seemed lost. They didn't work. Nothing worked, except his eyes, no air to breathe, no ears to hear. More pain.

No, he thought. This is not happening. We will reach Australia! Keep thinking of Australia ...

I will open my eyes and I'll be safe, he thought. I will be in Australia, in my room. Safe in bed, a real bed.

And then darkness.

CHAPTER 2

The bed was soft. The sheets smelled of sunlight, soft on his skin.

Faris opened his eyes.

The room was white. The striped curtains on the wide window looked out onto palm trees and a pure blue sky. A big bookcase stood full of books; the desk held the latest model computer; and there was a bright blue-and-red carpet on the white-tiled floor.

His bedroom, here in Australia.

Something niggled him, like a mouse nibbling a loaf of bread. A boat. A wave, cold against his skin. For a second his body was a balloon, about to burst, wanting to scream for air, but if he opened his mouth the water would pour through his body ...

No! There was no darkness here. No wave. Faris kept his eyes wide open, in case shutting them would bring the darkness back. He looked at the clock on the bedside table. Ten o'clock! He was late for school.

'Ah, the king of sleep wakes up.' Jadda appeared in the doorway. She wore her favourite red dress and gold combs in her black hair. 'It's good there is no school today. The teachers would be weeping, "Where is Faris? We can't have maths class without Faris to correct our mistakes."'

Faris laughed. He swung his legs out of bed. He grabbed the jeans and T-shirt from the chair by the desk. They felt crisp and new. He patted the computer. Its screen shone. He went to the blue-tiled bathroom and turned on the silver tap. Water gushed into the bath. Green water, bubbles above his head. Water that crushed him down ...

This was Australia! Australia where the water was clean and tame as it trickled into the tub. The wave had never happened. *But it did*, said a whisper in his brain. *It happened. It is still happening ...*

No! Faris forced himself to see the clean water fill the bath. The wave was in the past. Yes, that was a safe place to put it. In the past where it should be forgotten. He stepped into the warm bath. It smelled of orange blossom.

Breakfast was ready when he came out, his hair damp. It was the Australian buffet breakfast they had every day: food laid out on a long table — sliced chicken and fluffy bread rolls, red-cheeked peaches in a bowl of ice, a pineapple, a big cold fish and bowl after bowl of salad — in a room of tall windows.

For a moment — just a moment — he longed for another breakfast, for soft flat bread and ...

'Eat,' commanded Jadda. She sat at the table opposite him and smiled as he piled food on his plate from the buffet: orange salad with chopped onions and sliced cold chicken.

Something scratched at the door. Jadda grinned. 'Someone else demands his breakfast too.' She opened the door. A fat koala sat on the doorstep, its arms folded against its furry chest. It looked annoyed.

'Nosey! Have we neglected you?' Jadda picked up the koala.

It growled. 'Gffrff.'

Jadda laughed. She sat the koala on her lap and fed it lettuce leaves, then a chicken leg. The koala grasped the chicken leg in its furry hand, gnawing the meat, muttering contentedly.

Faris had thought he was hungry. But the food seemed strangely tasteless, even the pineapple, when he cut off the top and spooned out the inside as though it was a boiled egg.

Something nibbled at his brain again. He reached for it tentatively. His father! He was in Australia, so his father should be here.

He relaxed as he found an answer for that too. It was ten-thirty in the morning. His father was at work at the hospital.

'Now, go and play,' ordered Jadda. 'No books today.' She gave him a look. 'And no computer either. Today belongs to the beach.'

Faris grinned. Before breakfast he had longed to turn the computer on, to wander from topic to topic, a highway of knowledge, one question leading to another. But Jadda was right. He wanted to be at the beach today, the bright Australian beach.

He kissed her cheek, smelling the perfumed oil she used on her hair, her hand cream, the special scent that was Jadda alone. He opened the front door.

17

Green-and-red birds sang in a garden of red flowers and green leaves. A small fountain bubbled by the orange trees. The world smelled of roses and orange blossom.

Jadda saw his look. 'Paradise is a garden,' she said softly. 'Now down to the beach, with your friends.'

CHAPTER 3

He knew what the street would look like before he stepped through their front gate. Of course I know what it will look like, he told himself. I have been here before.

The houses stretched down the street, two-storey houses with bright green grass and rose bushes and orange trees laden with fruit. Each house had a car outside its garage, a new car that shone under the blue sky. Kangaroos munched peacefully. One peered up at him curiously as he passed.

Faris smiled as the road curved around the corner towards the beach. Two more houses and then a sand hill, hot dry pale sand tufted with tussocks and small spreading bushes, rising too high to see the sea.

The beach would be over the sand hill. Golden sand would stretch to the horizon, with dark green forest on one side and blue waves on the other. There would be young couples wandering hand in hand, the men in shorts and flowered shirts, the women in flowered sarongs. They would be barefoot. In Australia it wasn't rude to go barefoot on the beach.

Faris bent and unlaced his joggers. He left them neatly at the base of the sand hill and clambered up what was almost a path. Other feet had trudged this way before him. The sand was dry, breathing heat onto his skin. At last he reached the top.

And there was the beach, curved like a smile between two rocky headlands. He felt a faint surprise at its beauty, then shock ...

This wasn't his beach! He had never seen this beach before.

It was a small beach, ending in two jagged cliffs of tumbled black rocks at either end. Six great stones rose like giant's teeth across the small bay, with a few metres of rippled blue water between each of them. Small waves purred a little way up the beach, then slipped back, leaving the shine of water on the sand.

No crowds, no beach chairs, no couples looking into each other's eyes. This beach almost felt wild, as though few had ever trodden it. It was so clean it seemed to glow, the neat waves as blue as the sea further out. The only signs of civilisation were an old doorframe jammed up between the rocks below the nearest headland — washed in by the sea perhaps — and the prints of children's feet.

And laughter. Down on the sand two boys and two girls tossed a ball to each other. A little boy with black hair sat nearby, building a giant castle on the sand.

Faris stared at the group, shocked. He had never played with girls, certainly not like this.

The oldest girl wore a modest shawl in green and gold tucked around her head and shoulders, and bright green pants and a long shirt. The young girl was about ten. She was bareheaded, with her hair in two red plaits. Her shabby knitted shawl and long dress and apron hung almost to her ankles.

The older boy stood in the middle of the group, as though he controlled the game. He looked to be about fifteen and was short and stocky, in too-bright red trousers and a blue shirt. He had the whitest skin Faris had ever seen.

The other boy was about Faris's age. He too had white, white skin, though not leached of all colour as the older boy's. He wore a strange woollen suit, with short pants and long grey socks. No one wore flowered shirts, sarongs.

But this beach held something even more shocking than boys and girls playing together.

At the far end of the beach a dark-skinned young man waded knee-deep in the water, holding a fishing spear. He was naked. Naked in Australia! No clothes at all except for a string about his waist, with what looked like a stone knife dangling from it.

Faris gulped.

A dark-skinned young woman sat on the sand, watching the young man fish in the waves. She wore two pieces of what looked like soft furry leather, one tied about her top and the other like a tiny skirt. Strands of beads and tiny feathers hung about her neck. Tiny bright feathers were plaited into her hair.

Faris tried to force his eyes away. He had never seen a girl show so much of her body, or a woman either, except in the medical book his father had shown him, so many years before he could hardly remember what they looked like. Some of the boys at school had tried to find naked people on the internet, or girls in underwear or bathing costumes called bikinis. But of course those sites were blocked, as they should be blocked. Naked people should not be seen.

He should find another beach. *His* beach, the one he dreamed of. A true Australian beach ...

It was too late. The boy in red trousers had seen him. The boy shouted. The words were carried away by the sea wind, so Faris couldn't make them out. But suddenly the game below stopped.

The players turned to look at him.

If he left now, he'd look like a coward.

The boy in red gave a high and lazy toss of the ball, over the heads of the other players. The older girl leaped up and caught it. She looked at Faris curiously as the older boy jogged towards him The others stared too. Only the girl in the shawl smiled at him and waved. Her smile looked like a small sun of welcome.

The stocky boy in red drew closer. His eyes were blue. The white-mouse colour of his skin under too-long brown hair looked even more startling close up.

'A new cove! How's things, matey? I'm Billy Higgs.' The words were friendly, but there was a challenge like steel too.

'I'm Faris,' said Faris. He tried to keep his gaze away from the near-naked girl.

Billy grinned, showing a gap in yellow teeth. 'Far Eyes.'

'I'm sorry,' said Faris politely. 'I don't understand.'

'Your name. It's Far Eyes.'

'Faris,' corrected Faris.

22

Billy's grin didn't change. 'If I say your name is "Far Eyes", then that's what it is. On this beach I'm king. You understand?'

Faris nodded slowly. I should leave, he thought. Find *my* beach.

He didn't move.

Billy nodded, as though satisfied. 'Two more laws then. No questions. Not on my beach. You takes us as you find us.'

'What's the second law?'

The grin had gone now. Billy stared at him, intent. 'We don't speak of the past on this beach. None of us. Never. We're here to enjoy ourselves, an' that's what we do.' The grin returned. 'It's good here, matey. The rules keeps it good for everyone. Now are y' stayin'? Or goin'?'

How long had it been since Faris had played with friends? How long since a day had been simply for fun?

A small flock of red-and-green birds flew above them, making dapples on the golden sand. The wind blew, warm from the land and the sun. The waves here were blue, gentle as curtains. Suddenly he knew that laughter and sunlight would drive away all thoughts of dark waves and tumbling water.

'Staying,' said Faris. He followed Billy across the sand.

CHAPTER 4

The game stopped as Faris and Billy drew close. The little girl in the apron and knitted shawl who had waved stepped towards them.

'Hello,' she said. The freckles on her nose danced as she smiled. 'I'm Susannah. It's grand to have you join us.' Her voice had a strange music to it.

'This is Far Eyes.' Billy glanced at Faris, as though daring him to correct him.

'I'm Jamila.' The girl in the head shawl looked down politely as she spoke. Faris wondered if Jamila also knew that a modest girl shouldn't play with boys on a beach.

'That there is David,' said Billy. The boy in the strange short woollen suit gave a small bow.

Faris nodded. 'Hello.'

'And the little cove building the sandcastle is Nikko. He's always building sandcastles,' added Billy. His voice almost sounded indulgent. 'Ever since Mei Ling showed him how to.'

'Who is Mei Ling?' asked Faris. Surely the near-naked dark-skinned girl wasn't called Mei Ling.

'Mei Ling ain't here no more,' said Billy curtly. 'No questions. Remember?' The blue eyes stared at him. Faris felt fear whisper through his belly. What would

Billy do if he broke the rules? Tell him to leave? Hit him, or ...

'Catch!' said Jamila suddenly. She threw the ball hard and high, over Billy's head. David, the woollen-suit boy, leaped up to grab it. He looked around, then threw the ball to Susannah. Billy jumped. His white hands grabbed the ball before Susannah could catch it.

Susannah laughed. Faris's fear vanished in the breeze. Billy held the ball, calculating for a moment, then threw the ball above Faris's head to David again.

It took Faris five minutes to learn the game, to see that there were no rules, as such. You threw the ball to whoever was furthest from you, and leaped high to catch it before someone else could.

Billy was in the middle, always in the middle. No one ever threw the ball to Billy, but half the time he caught it anyway, snatching it from the air, crowing with laughter, circling his white feet on the sand till he chose someone to throw it to.

The fourth time Billy caught the ball he grinned at Faris. 'Hey, Far Eyes.' Suddenly the ball headed across the others' heads. Faris jumped to catch it. Its force knocked him onto the sand. He scrambled up, winded. Had Billy meant to hurt him?

'Grand catch!' yelled Billy.

Faris grinned. It *had* been a good catch, especially for a boy who had never played a game like this before. He looked at the ball more closely. It was made of leather, brown and roughly stitched.

He hesitated, wondering who to throw the ball to next, trying not to keep glancing at the naked young man and the near-naked young woman, now kneeling by a smoky fire further down the beach. Billy hadn't mentioned their names and for now, at least, Faris would keep Billy's rules. No questions.

Two silver-scaled fish lay in the sand beside the fire. Faris could smell smoke, sweet above the scents of salt and seaweed.

'Come on, Far Eyes! Throw!' yelled Billy.

At last Faris chose little Susannah. There was something about her eyes — cloudless eyes that looked straight at him. It should have looked immodest, a girl staring like that at a boy. But instead it just felt as if she truly saw him …

He thrust the thought away and threw the ball. It soared above Billy in the middle. It was going to pass over Susannah as well. To his delight Susannah ran backwards on the sand, grabbed it with a laugh, then tossed it to the almost naked black girl, who had jogged up behind.

And suddenly the girl's bare black body didn't matter, nor did Billy the bully. The shadows of the wave disappeared too. There was just the game, the sunlight, the laughter.

The ball flashed across the deep blue sky. Slowly Faris began to learn how the others played. Jamila caught the ball as though she had never known that women shouldn't shove their way past men — or perhaps she, like Jadda, had deliberately forgotten. Thin David in his woollen suit played as though his mind was somewhere else. Billy threw the ball with strength and laughter. But the laughter seemed to tell everyone that he was in control.

The sun was high when Jamila and Susannah vanished over the sand hill. Susannah's shawl flapped in the breeze. She came back lugging a giant basket and a stone flagon in the other hand. Jamila walked a little way behind, carrying a tall silver jug and a cloth.

Faris ran to help with the basket. Susannah grinned at him. 'A gentleman you are indeed. Thank you.'

Faris took the basket and peered down into it. It was filled with packages wrapped in clean white cloth.

'Enough for everyone,' said Susannah proudly. 'All the food we can eat.' She hesitated. 'You like cheese, don't you?'

Faris nodded. Susannah smiled. Her teeth were crooked, but it was the kindest smile Faris had ever seen. 'We have to be careful what we bring to the beach. Jamila can't eat pork, nor David neither, and he can't eat meat and butter at the same time. And some people bring down the strangest things! Henri brought down frogs' legs. Eating frogs' legs! Can you believe it now?'

Faris wrinkled his nose at the idea of frogs' legs. 'Maybe it was a joke. Does Henri come down to the beach often?'

'He's gone,' said Jamila shortly.

Where had Henri gone to? But Billy had said 'no questions'. Faris glanced at Billy. He and the other two players had gathered around the young black couple's fire.

'Nikko!' Susannah called to the littlest boy. 'Come and eat!' She held out her hand as he ran towards her and Jamila.

Faris walked with them over to the fire. Sticks with flesh threaded onto them sat suspended over the flames. Faris could smell fish cooking.

The young black man stood up, as though he was giving them permission to sit by his fire. Almost, thought Faris, as he looked at the pride in the strong straight back, as though he owned the beach.

Suddenly, despite Billy's claim and the young man's nakedness, the black man looked to be the beach's true king, not Billy.

'This is Far Eyes,' said Billy, behind him. 'Far Eyes, this is Mudurra.'

Mudurra nodded, without speaking. He sat down on the sand again. He held out his hands as Jamila knelt and poured water over them. She handed Mudurra the cloth, then moved to pour water over Billy's hands, then Susannah's and the others.

Faris held out his hands too. It was a familiar enough ritual, but felt strange here on an Australian beach. The water smelled of roses. He waited to see if there would be prayer before the meal too. Jadda had said that there were no prayers in public in Australia, that most Australians never prayed at all. I'm not scared of Billy, he told himself. I just don't want to offend.

Instead Mudurra picked up one of the half-blackened fish sticks and handed it to the near-naked young woman. She flashed him a smile of thanks, then looked at Faris. 'I'm Juhi.'

Faris tried not to look at Juhi's bare skin. 'Hello.'

Juhi blew on the fish to cool it, then broke off a piece to eat. She ate neatly, using only her right hand. Susannah unwrapped the packages.

There were sandwiches, thick hunks of soft white bread spread with butter and filled with yellow cheese, and chunks of a strange dark brown cake that tasted of fruit and spices.

'Eat up,' said Susannah. Faris hid a smile. She sounded as old as Jadda, more like a grandma than a little girl.

It was so good that Faris had eaten three sandwiches, and two slices of the cake, before he realised that all the others were eating as silently and as intently as him, sandwich after sandwich, slice after slice of cake.

'Here.' Dark hands passed him a stick holding slightly blackened fish strips.

He looked up to see Mudurra grinning at him. 'Thank you.' The fish flaked in Faris's fingers, sweet and moist, tasting of the sea, the calm blue sea of the beach, not a black wave that …

He shut his mind to the thought as Susannah passed him the stone flagon.

He hesitated. He'd never shared a drinking glass, much less drunk from a shared container. You might catch someone's germs or viruses. Susannah looked at him with concern. 'It's good,' she reassured him. 'You need to drink after a morning in the sun.'

Mudurra laughed. He offered Faris something like a big wrinkled balloon instead.

Faris tried to hide his disgust. The wrinkled balloon must be a water bladder made from animal guts. He had seen them on TV, tied with a kind of string at both ends. He shook his head, he hoped politely, and took a sip from the flagon instead.

It was buttermilk, cold and both slightly sour and sweet. He drank till he had had enough, then passed it on.

At last the food was gone. Susannah folded the white cloths, and put the flagon and Jamila's silver jug and cloth in the basket. She carried it across the sand as the wind swept at her skirts and shawl and apron.

Billy stood, carrying the ball. The others followed him, away from the fire. They began to play the game again, Mudurra and Juhi and even little Nikko too. When Faris looked up, Susannah was sitting halfway up the sand hill, her basket beside her.

Was she watching the waves, Faris wondered, or wondering if a ship would sail by?

No. Susannah was watching them. Like a grandmother, making sure we're safe, thought Faris. But that was silly. Susannah was just a little girl. And there was nothing dangerous here. Was there?

The game continued. Throw and catch, and throw and catch. Billy still grabbed most balls. Faris looked at Mudurra. The naked young man had a smile about his eyes.

Mudurra could catch every ball, thought Faris. He is taller and stronger than Billy. But he lets Billy win. He allows Billy to be king.

The sun shifted in the sky. The breeze blew cool. All at once Faris realised it must be late afternoon, that one by one the players were leaving, trudging up the sand hill by themselves. David, the boy in the strange short woollen suit, had already vanished, and tiny Nikko. Now Jamila began to walk up the beach. She sang as she walked. The wind grabbed her words and twisted them, impossible to understand. Then she was gone, over the sand hill. Only Billy and the black couple were on the beach now.

'I'd better go home,' said Faris. Billy nodded, as though Faris had asked permission, then threw the ball to Mudurra, who threw it to Juhi.

Faris trudged up the sand hill in silence, aware that Susannah was still watching him from halfway up its slope. Her legs were drawn up under her thick skirts and apron, as though she had sat here on the sand hill many times before.

He'd have to walk past her to get down to the road.

It wasn't right to talk to a girl alone unless she was a member of your family, even one as young as Susannah. He gave Susannah a brief nod and walked past her.

'Wait!' she called after him. 'Can you sit a minute?' Her eyes were green, like the grass the kangaroos munched.

Her words were soft and sympathetic. Yet despite her quiet tone, Faris found himself obeying as though she had ordered him. He sat next to her, embarrassed, looking at the players down on the sand instead of at her.

Susannah smiled again. Some people had empty smiles. Susannah's was full of caring. 'What's your name?'

He glanced at her, surprised. Susannah grinned, showing her crooked teeth. She almost looked like an ordinary ten-year-old when she grinned. 'I know it isn't Far Eyes,' she added. The music in her voice was stronger than ever.

'I thought Billy didn't let us ask questions.'

'Not on the beach. But this is the sand hill.'

Faris glanced down at Billy. He had the feeling that the big boy was carefully not watching what happened up here.

'What is your real name?' insisted Susannah.

'It's Faris.'

She pulled a small leather-covered notebook from the pocket of her apron and a stub of pencil. 'How would you be spelling that then?'

'F. A. R. I. S.'

Susannah wrote carefully and slowly. She glanced up and smiled again. 'My mam taught me my letters,' she said proudly. 'I can figure too, but not as well.'

'Figure?'

'You know. Add the numbers up. I can count up to a hundred too.'

'That's excellent,' Faris said politely, thinking, Stupid, to be ten years old and know so little. He looked over Susannah's shoulder at the page she was writing on. It was a long list of names. Names covered the page on the other side too.

'I keep the names of everyone who comes to the

beach,' she explained. 'See, that's you there.' She pointed to the last name on the list. 'And there's my name, Susannah.' She pointed to the round letters near the bottom of the first page.

Faris looked at the list. Mudurra's name was the first, then someone called Ah Goon, then Pedro, Jan and Henri. Billy's name was near the top too. There were many other names, not just the names of those he'd met today: Mei Ling, Bridget, Jane, Vlad ... But he had enough names to keep straight already.

'Susannah's a lovely name,' he said instead.

Susannah smiled. 'It is the loveliest name I know.'

'Why do you talk so funny?' He hadn't meant to say it, but Susannah laughed.

'Oh, that's the Irish accent. I come from Ireland, you see.'

'Before you came to Australia?'

She looked at him seriously, then nodded. 'Before I came to Australia. The others on the beach complained about the accent at first. But you'll get used to it. And where do you come from?' she added, her voice just slightly too casual.

'I'm from ...' He stopped. He couldn't remember. No, he didn't *want* to remember. Billy was right, not this small girl with impudent eyes and questions. This was a place to be happy, not to remember. Suddenly he too wanted a world with no questions.

'What does it matter?' he asked roughly.

'No matter,' Susannah said gently. 'No matter at all.'

Somehow he lost his anger. Susannah stood up. For a moment Faris thought she was going to hug him. He didn't want to be hugged by a strange girl. But all she said was, 'I'll be seeing you tomorrow then, will I?'

Did he really want to come to the beach again, with bare black skin and impudent girls, to be bullied by Billy? He nodded anyway. He stepped up to the top of the sand hill, then stared down at the landscape beyond.

This wasn't his street! It was a dirt track lined with stone houses with tiled roofs in big gardens — so big they were not like gardens at all — rows of vegetables, like tiny farms. And cows! A fat cow in every garden, and over there a sheep, so white it looked as though it had been washed!

In its own strange way the world below was beautiful, despite the dusty road: the way a movie could be lovely, but you wouldn't want to live inside it. Enormous blue butterflies fluttered over the vegetables. A cat yawned, comfortable, on a windowsill. The chimneys all puffed smoke.

But the cows! The vegetables, right in the front garden! This was a land for peasants!

It was impossible that this street could be anywhere near the street he'd walked along this morning. There weren't even any streetlights or cars at all, not even what might be a garage. He glanced back at Susannah. 'I … I think I'm lost.'

She touched his hand quickly. 'Don't you be scared.'

He snatched his hand away. 'I'm not scared!'

'Of course you're not,' she said quietly. 'It's my fault. I shouldn't be standing here with you, especially not on your first day here. Go down to the beach again, then walk back up the sand hill. You'll find your own road waiting for you when you get back up here.'

'I don't understand.' How could he have got lost just going up a sand hill? And how could this little girl be so sure he'd find the right street again? He looked at Susannah uncertainly.

'It's a rule, if you like. Always walk across the sand hill by yourself. I'll go home now, to make sure it goes right for you. Don't worry. This is a good place, a safe place. Nothing bad can come to you here. Nothing at all. Good night, Faris.'

Susannah smiled again. She picked up her basket, then headed down the sand hill towards the house with the cat on the windowsill. As Faris watched, a lamp shone in one of the windows. A door opened. He heard children's laughter.

He shook his head. Australian cattle lived on great big 'stations' where they were rounded up with helicopters. He looked down again. Susannah had vanished into the house now. He could smell wood smoke and what he thought must be cow.

Maybe Susannah lives in a theme park, he told himself. Australia had many theme parks: Water Worlds and Fun Worlds and Movie Worlds. Maybe this was part of a Movie World. Relief filled him. That had to be the answer. Susannah's father must work there.

A good place. A safe place. Susannah's words hung in his head.

The important thing now was to find his own street. Perhaps if he walked along the sand hill he'd see where it began. He hesitated, then decided to do what Susannah had suggested. She was young, but there had been a certainty about her. A kindness too, as though she almost knew what he was feeling.

Happiness, Faris told himself. He felt happy. He'd had a day at the beach. A good day, in spite of Billy. A day of sunlight and laughter. Jadda would be waiting at home ... He found himself walking back down the sand hill to the beach, just as Susannah had told him to — a little girl ordering an older boy! He turned and clambered up it again.

The breeze from the sea was cool on his skin.

And there was his street below him, the comfortable two-storey homes with their gardens and bright streetlights. The kangaroos had vanished, off to sleep wherever kangaroos slept.

Faris tried to tell his heart to stop thudding. He'd come up the same track. This was impossible! It was all impossible, the sunlight and the laughter ...

No. He was tired, that was all. Confused because he was tired after a day in the sun. *You must believe that everything is possible*, said Jadda's whisper in his mind.

Faris ran down the sand hill. He put on his joggers, then ran along the street. The scents of roses and orange blossom were joined by the scents of baking bread now, and roasting meat, and the clean, exciting, almost electric smell that you sniffed, just for a moment, when you opened the box of a new laptop computer or mobile phone.

Faris smiled. Of course Australia smelled like this. A new country would smell new too.

Jadda opened the door. She wore her old dressing gown and carried the book she had been reading, a Jane Austen one. She folded him into her warmth and perfume. 'How was your day?'

'Good.' Faris nodded at the book. 'You should read an Australian book now.'

'Ah, but this is about Jane Austen's visit to Australia. It even has kangaroos! Come on. Dinner is ready.'

All at once he didn't want Australian food, the bright buffet with too many dishes.

'Mutton soup with lentils,' said Jadda softly, as if she understood just what he felt. 'And coconut cake.'

His favourite. I must take Jadda's cake down to the beach, he thought. His new friends would like Jadda's coconut cake.

'Your father has to work late,' said Jadda. 'We won't wait for him.' She led Faris into the bright house, with its smells of cooking and orange blossom from the trees outside.

Faris was tired when he lay down that night. And happy, he told himself. But for some reason he didn't want to turn off the light. Dreams came in darkness. Dreams of a giant wave that towered above him, of trying to breathe and finding only water ...

It wasn't real. *This* was real! The warm bed, the perfect bedroom, just as he had always imagined it.

Exactly as he had imagined it. For one frozen moment he wondered if his bedroom might be a dream, if when he shut his eyes he would really be opening them.

And then he remembered the beach. He had never imagined a beach like that, with its rocks like a gap-toothed smile. He could never imagine anyone like Billy either, with his mouse-white skin, or Mudurra naked with his spear, Jamila's song or even Susannah with her kind eyes and shawl.

If he could never imagine them, then they had to be real. If they were real, then he was safe. I can sleep, he told himself, and my dreams will be good dreams.

He switched off the light and held his breath.

The computer shone dimly in the moonlight from the window. He shut his eyes and let sleep take him. Soft sleep, gentle sleep, with no dreams of waves and thrashing water.

CHAPTER 5

It was a holiday the next day too.

'Go down to the beach,' urged Jadda. 'Go and laugh in the sun with your friends.'

Faris nodded. He left her sitting on the cushions, with the koala in her lap and Jane Austen in her hands. But when he got to the street he stopped.

Yesterday had been too strange. He had enjoyed the time on the beach, except for Billy's bossiness. He had almost got used to Mudurra's nakedness and Juhi's too-much-bare skin.

But when he had looked over the sand hill and seen cottages and cows, not his familiar street, he had been frightened. No, not frightened, he told himself. This was Australia! There was nothing to be frightened of here.

He would go for a walk along the streets. He might find Susannah's dirt road. Maybe he would find another beach. A proper Australian beach with holiday-makers in flowered shirts, and a big blue swimming pool so you didn't have to go near the waves.

He turned away from the route to the beach. Along one road, then round a corner, then along the next road. Each house looked like the ones in his street, all two storeys, with smart garages. Some had cars, and one had a boat parked outside on a trailer. Another had a tennis court, and there were different trees and flowers in their gardens.

All were beautiful.

Mobs of kangaroos rested in the shade of the trees, or reached up to pick figs or oranges from the trees. Faris turned another corner and stopped.

His home gazed at him from across the street.

It was impossible! He'd travelled away from his home. He was sure he had.

But he'd been dreaming of beaches and swimming pools. He set out again. This time he made sure he turned away from his house at each corner. One street, another ...

He knew a second before he saw it. There was his own house. The koala dozed on the doorstep, its fat tummy full of toast and chicken.

Faris stumbled past it, through the front door.

Jadda looked up from her book. 'Faris, what is it? Was the sun too hot?'

'I didn't go down to the beach. I'm fine,' he added roughly. 'I'm going to my room, to use the computer.'

Jadda looked at him seriously. 'I think you should go to the beach.'

Go to the beach. Go to the beach, said that small whisper in Faris's mind.

He ignored it. He wanted to use the computer! He loved computers. He could go to the beach tomorrow.

He shut his bedroom door and sat at his desk. The computer stared at him. He reached to turn it on, then hesitated. It was almost as if his hand didn't want to press the 'on' switch.

This was silly. He reached over to the switch again.

Someone knocked at the front door. Faris stood up in relief. (No, not relief, he told himself. Why shouldn't he turn on his computer?)

Jadda had opened the door. The koala had vanished. Susannah stood on the doorstep. She looked even more out of place in the neat doorway, with the flowers behind her, standing there in her long apron with her shabby shawl. He flushed, embarrassed that Jadda would think he had a friend like this, a little girl.

But Jadda didn't seem to notice any strangeness. 'Are you looking for Faris?'

Susannah nodded. She looked at him past Jadda. 'Please come to the beach,' she said.

'Why?' asked Faris roughly. He waited for Jadda to whisper to him, 'Be polite.' But she didn't.

Susannah met his gaze with her clear one. 'Because the beach is where you need to be. We need you,' she added.

'To play the game?' He supposed the game was more interesting with more players.

'For that too.'

Suddenly he longed to be there: the clean sand, the laughter. Even the rocks called to him.

Jadda smiled. 'Have fun, my dear one,' she said.

Faris walked side by side with Susannah, down the road to the beach. He hoped none of the neighbours would look out and see him walking with a little girl. But no one appeared.

They climbed the sand hill together. And suddenly there was the beach, as bright as yesterday, almost glowing in the sun. Billy waved up at them. Jamila and David waved too, and little Nikko. Even Juhi smiled at him, as she sat on the sand, near Mudurra swimming in the soft blue sea, his body spearing back to shore on a neat white-laced wave till he landed on his stomach in the shallows.

Faris tried not to look at him. It wasn't the lack of clothes that made him uncomfortable today. It was the waves. Those waves that washed the golden sand could also be monsters that clutched you and pulled you down ...

A gate shut in his mind. What had Billy said yesterday? *We don't speak of the past on this beach.* Billy's right, he thought. Forget the pain of yesterdays. Think of the now, the bright day that was Australia.

The sand was warm under his feet as he followed Susannah down the sand hill. 'Catch, Far Eyes!' yelled Billy. The ball soared towards him.

It was good to be part of the laughter, to think of nothing but the warm sand and the game. He was even better at it today, able to throw the ball up and over to Susannah or David, out of Billy's reach nearly every time.

It was a good game. Good to be with friends. Good to be warm and well fed, to know that Jadda was at home, their clean bright home. Why had he tried to go for a walk today instead of coming here? Yet even as he thought it, he found himself wandering away from the game, along the beach towards the headland.

'Oi! You! Far Eyes!' Billy grabbed his shoulder. 'Where you goin'?'

Faris looked at him, puzzled by his anger. 'Just down the beach.'

'No one walks this far down the beach without my say-so.' Billy's grasp tightened on his shoulder. It hurt.

Faris tried to pull his arm away. 'Is that another rule? Mudurra comes down here!'

'You ain't Mudurra.'

'Let him go.'

Susannah stood with her hands on her hips, her green eyes firm. Faris waited for Billy to yell at her, even to hit her. He tensed, ready to hit the older boy back.

Instead Billy met Susannah's gaze. 'He shouldn't go wanderin' off.'

'It's his choice, Billy.'

Billy brushed Faris's arm away. 'Go on. Go for your walk along the beach then, Far Eyes. We'll be waiting for you.' He strode back to the game.

Faris didn't want to walk now. But it would be embarrassing to go back. He glanced at Susannah, shrugged and began to walk again along the beach.

There wasn't much to see. The waves lashed at the headland, making it impossible to climb around. The only remarkable thing was the doorframe, propped between the rocks. It wasn't a proper door, as he had thought, but two ancient logs of driftwood, coming together in a rough arch at the top, their lower ends buried in the sand. A weathered skin hung between them so you couldn't see behind.

Faris touched the skin. It felt cold, despite the sunlight and the hot and crinkly sand under his feet. His fingers pushed …

The world was dark and wet and cold. He shuddered, drew his hand back, blinked.

He was warm and dry on the sunny beach again.

'There now, it's all right. You're safe here.' Susannah had followed him. She gave him a quick hug. It felt wrong, being touched by a girl he wasn't related to, who talked to him like he was the child, instead of older than her. 'Come back to the game again.'

He stepped away from her. 'I … I was cold.'

'Were you? Don't worry yourself. You can come back to the door tomorrow, or the next day maybe.'

Why would he want to come back to an old doorway on a beach?

He glanced at it.

'Next week maybe,' said Susannah. 'No hurry. No hurry in the world.'

He walked with her back along the beach.

CHAPTER 6

He didn't go for a walk through the streets again. He didn't walk along the beach to the door either.

Days passed. Good days, with no strangeness. A world of sunlight and the beach.

Every morning the game and his new friends waited for him, and the golden sand and neat waves, the black cliffs on either side, the rocks that grinned at him from between the headlands. Sometimes a seabird sat on them, but mostly they shone smooth and bare from the polishing of water.

Billy had never threatened him again, though sometimes Faris felt the older boy watching him. Susannah watched too from the sand hill each afternoon. Her watching felt different.

Every lunchtime Jamila washed their hands. Someone brought down food — so much food, and yet each time every last bite was eaten. David brought a big pot of beef, cooked with sweet prunes and carrots, and boxes of chocolates, with creamy centres. Susannah poked the centre out with her tongue before she nibbled the outside.

Jamila brought great pans of spiced mutton stew, piled so high the meat juice spilled onto the sand, and fresh bread, still hot from the oven, and pomegranates, cold from the fridge. Billy lugged down legs of cold meat, beef and mutton, hot pies with gravy, apple pie and giant loaves of black-topped bread. He grinned as he handed round the food. Faris almost liked him then.

Juhi brought grapes, salads of parsley and mint and grains, pastries with spicy fillings and flat strange spongy bread to dip into oily stews. Once even little Nikko lugged down a massive black pot filled with a thick stew of lamb and tomatoes and potatoes.

Only Mudurra never brought food down the sand hill. Mudurra conjured food from the beach — the fish he cooked on his smouldering driftwood fire; skittering crabs that danced above the waterline till his quick fingers grabbed them, with shells that turned deep red as they cooked on the coals. Sometimes Mudurra found shellfish on the rocks by the cliffs, or dug strange tubers from the sand hill that he cooked near the coals of the fire; they were fibrous but sweet and so hot they burned your tongue. Each day Mudurra gave a fish to Juhi first, before he fed the others. She ate it with her long black fingers and perfect white teeth.

There was buttermilk to drink, or almond milk, pomegranate or apple juice in big jugs, or water from the bladders that Mudurra filled from a spring that oozed fresh water near the base of the sand hill.

No one brought Australian food. There were no big platters of cold chicken, no pineapples, no giant bowls of fruit salad or pavlova topped with passionfruit, no lamingtons or pumpkin scones or seared barramundi with chilli jam.

Some days Faris thought he would bring everyone proper Australian food from his big breakfast buffet. But somehow, when it felt right that he be the one to go home to fetch their midday meal, he found himself offering Jadda's bean soup, her coconut cake and the salad she made with red onions and pomegranates that crunched sweetness onto your tongue.

Each day had a routine now. He would go to the beach, and the others would be there. Billy and Susannah were always there when he arrived, throwing the ball to each other, waving happily as he appeared. Mudurra and Juhi were always there too, Mudurra fishing with his long sharp spear, Juhi watching him, or sometimes searching along the beach for driftwood for the fire.

Faris and Susannah, Billy, Jamila and David would spend the whole morning playing the game, while little Nikko built sandcastles or dug great holes to see them fill with water, though sometimes he joined the game too. Even Billy was careful to throw gently to the little boy.

When the sun glared high above them, they ate their food, then Susannah left to watch them from the sand hill, and Mudurra and Juhi joined the game. The game was always faster and more furious when the dark-skinned couple played, with more laughter too.

Then, as the sun dipped down towards the sand hill, one by one they left the beach.

David always left first, in his short woollen suit and long socks and polished shoes. Sometimes Jamila followed him, her shawl neat about her head, singing

47

her song with the wind, its words lost among the lap of waves. Nikko left early too, his tiny body weary, pausing on the sand hill for Susannah to give him a quick kiss before patting him on his way.

Sometimes Faris left after lunch too. He curled up on the cushions in their house while Jadda read to him, not Australian books but the old stories from when he was small, which for some reason were all he wanted to listen to now. Other times he waited till the sun dropped low behind the sand hill, turning the sky pink and red and orange, till the shadows thickened on the beach, and Billy said, 'Hey, matey. It's time to go.'

Faris was careful now to go up the sand hill alone, just like the others did, just as Susannah had said. He didn't know why he obeyed her. Surely he'd just got lost that time he'd looked down on the farm-like gardens and dirt track? But everyone walked up the sand hill alone. It seemed as important as not asking questions on the beach.

No matter how late Faris stayed, Mudurra and Juhi were always still on the shore. Perhaps, he thought, they lived there. But there was no sign of a shelter, or even furs or dry grass to make a bed.

Every night his street was waiting for him, the smell of orange blossom and the grazing kangaroos, and Jadda opening the front door, a smiling Jadda with her book in her hand, and the smell of bean soup behind her.

It was enough. All I want, he told himself. He had lived with fear so long (he shut his mind to what that fear had been, but the memory that he had been afraid lingered). This was a time for sunlight, for golden sand. This was a holiday.

This was Australia. This was peace. This was home, with Jadda and his father.

Though, of course, somehow his father was never there.

'He is working late tonight again,' said Jadda, when Faris asked where his father was, as he sat down at the table for his dinner.

You told me that last night, he thought. And the night before that. How many nights had his father worked late? How many mornings had Faris slept so long that his father was gone when he got up?

How long were school holidays in Australia?

There has been no Friday, he thought. No days of the week at all. No calls to prayer, no Ramadan, no holy days for any of the religions in Australia.

But this was Australia, where prayers and religion were private. They had prayed back home, but Faris had never known what Jadda thought of prayer, or even of religion. The only time he had asked her she had looked at him seriously and said, 'Ask me in a few years.' As though what she wanted to say was too big to voice yet.

He looked at Jadda, smiling at him, and somehow he couldn't ask about prayer, or even what day of the week it was. He could only drink his soup and eat his bread — the flat bread of home, not the puffy bread rolls from his buffet breakfast, nor the big black-topped bread or the round heavy loaves the others brought to the beach — sleep in his clean sheets, where no rats scuffled in the night, where no wave rose like a sea beast reaching up a hand from the endless black depths ...

He woke, sweating, then sat up in the darkness.

He was in a bed. A bed! And down the hall was Jadda, sleeping too. His father was in the room next door. Faris had only to walk down there and Jadda would wake and comfort him. He had only to open his father's door and he would see ...

What? What did his father look like?

Of course I know what my father looks like, he told himself. My father has ... He forced his memory back. Black hair, black beard, eyes that smiled as he watched his son read to him from a leather-covered book.

The face was vague, too far away.

He was being stupid. He had only to get up, go down the corridor, open his father's bedroom door. His father wouldn't be at the hospital now. Faris could wake him up, or look at him at least.

Get up, he told himself. Turn on the light, go out the door.

He stayed where he was, in the warm nest of bed. And, finally, he slept again.

CHAPTER 7

He left the game early the next afternoon, even before David. He had felt strange all day, as though he just floated in the world, as though there were shadows he couldn't see.

Too little sleep, Faris told himself. The nightmare had stolen sleep. He nodded to Susannah as he walked up the sand hill, hoping she'd let him pass without speaking.

'Going home?'

Again he was caught by the strange music of her voice. 'Yes.'

'Wait,' she said.

'What for? I'm tired.' Even as he said it, he knew he wasn't tired. Scared, perhaps, though he didn't know of what. Stop it, he told himself. What is there to be scared of? This is a happy place. There is nothing bad here.

'Because I'm thinking it's time you saw something. I'm thinking that you are ready for it now.' Susannah looked up at him, hugging her knees under her long dress and apron.

'Ready for what?'

'Sit down,' she ordered.

He sat, the dry sand warm under his jeans, resenting the way this small girl gave him orders, angry at himself, a little, for obeying them.

He knew nothing about her, he realised. Nothing about any of them, despite the days they'd played together. It wasn't just Billy's rule that had stopped him asking questions. It was as though his brain had been closed. Was it now slowly opening?

'You talk like you're almost singing.' He hadn't meant to say it. It sounded rude.

But instead of minding, Susannah laughed. 'Bridget always said my accent came from the Irish bogs.'

He thought of the other names Susannah had written in her book. There had been so many of them, but no one else ever came down to their beach, no adult, no other child. 'Who's Bridget?'

Susannah's face lost a little of its smile. 'She's gone now.'

'Gone where?'

'Now that,' she said, 'I can't be telling you. Home, I hope. A good home. Now here comes David.'

Faris watched the boy trudge up the sand hill. Susannah stood as he stopped to empty the sand out of his shiny black shoes. 'Ah, David. Do you mind if we come with you?'

Faris glanced at her, annoyed. He didn't want to go with David. He wanted to go home, to the familiar comfort of Jadda. They could sort through the lentils for stones together, just as they'd always done …

But it would be rude to contradict Susannah, an insult to David too.

David looked at his watch. It was a big one, old-fashioned, with hands instead of numbers. 'If you like. I have to hurry. They're waiting for me.'

'You go on ahead,' said Susannah gently. 'We'll see you there.'

David nodded. He laced up his shoes again, then stepped carefully up to the top of the sand hill.

'Are we going to his home?' called Faris, as Susannah followed David.

She shook her head. 'You'll see.'

Faris hauled himself to his feet and climbed to the top of the sand hill, where Susannah waited for him. He looked down at the street below.

A city street. But this was like no city he had ever seen, even on the internet.

Faris stared. There had been ... strange ... things. He could blank his mind to strange. But this was impossible.

These buildings were two and three storeys high. Most were shops, some with wide windows, others with funny windows made up of many small panes of glass. People in old-fashioned suits walked along the street. Strange cars moved slowly down the road, like those he had seen in a movie years ago, set in the middle of the last century.

Another set of Movie World, he told himself.

He didn't believe it. Nor could he believe that Susannah's cottage was a Movie World set.

He dug his fingers into his hands so hard the nails hurt. Was he going mad? His father had told him of a mentally ill patient at the hospital, who thought the trees spoke to him. Could a mental illness make you imagine a whole world?

'Where are we?' He tried to keep his voice steady. 'What's happening?'

'It's all right. Don't worry. I'll explain it all later.'

'Explain it now!'

'I can't. There's something you have to see first. Don't worry,' she added. 'It's a good thing to see. A wonderful one.'

'What?'

'You'll see.' Susannah tugged at his hand. She sounded patient. She sounded kind, as if she really was trying to show him what all the strangeness meant. If she had been rude or impudent, Faris could have turned his back on her, walked down the sand hill again, then back up to find his way home, leaving her behind.

But it was hard to turn his back on kindness.

He looked down at his bare feet. There was no sign of his shoes. He didn't want to walk down the street with bare feet, like an alley boy.

He hesitated, then followed Susannah dumbly onto the footpath, through the crowds of men and women.

The cement felt warm under his feet. But no one stared at him, even though the men wore woollen suits, though with long trousers, unlike David's short ones. Each man wore a hat too, not sun hats with 'Welcome to Queensland' on them, but grey or black felt. Every woman wore careful clothes: stockings, high-heeled shoes, gloves, hats with scraps of net, or bunches of fake flowers or cherries. And yet the well-dressed people didn't even glance at his jeans or Susannah's too-big, much-mended dress.

It was odd to be in a city again. How long had it been since he had seen any other adult than Jadda? These grown-ups were strangely quiet, with small quiet smiles.

He glanced at a shop as they passed it. It was a cake shop, but what cakes! Three or four layers high, oozing cream, topped with shaved chocolate. Others, smaller, filled with cream and strawberries, pastry in the shape of a curling wave, filled with cream too.

He stopped so suddenly, staring at the sheer quantity of pastry, that a man bumped into him. The man gave a slight bow, lifting his hat. '*Entschuldigen Sie mich bitte.*'

It wasn't English. It wasn't any language Faris recognised. He listened to the soft rumble of conversation around him. It sounded like the same language. Thanks to Jadda, he knew enough about languages to be able to distinguish one from another, even if he couldn't speak them.

If they were in Europe, he might have thought that they had crossed a border without his noticing. But Australia was one great splodge in the middle of the sea.

'Susannah! Wait! Where are we?'

'David's Australia.'

'There is only one Australia!'

Susannah twisted her way through the adult bodies as though she was used to it. 'You think everyone sees the world in the same way?'

55

It was a perceptive comment for a little girl to make, thought Faris, especially a child who had to sound out the letters as she wrote. Of course everyone saw the world differently. But not as differently as this.

He stared at the shops around them: nearest was a fruit shop, with piles of apples, a mound of bright oranges, small white sacks of cherries. 'We should go back. What if we get lost?'

'We won't.' She walked swiftly past a chocolate shop, the chocolates in vast tiers on silver dishes, dark ones and milk and white, boxes of pink Turkish delight, thick with pistachios, and nougat and bright-coloured squares and packages that Faris couldn't recognise, but still they somehow looked tempting, as though they'd melt in sweetness on your tongue.

Faris wondered if this was where David had bought the chocolates he'd brought to the beach, the ones Susannah loved.

'But what if ...?'

'Shh,' said Susannah. She hadn't even glanced at the chocolate shop, intent on following David through the crowd.

She really cares for David, thought Faris, but she doesn't look at him the way Juhi looks at Mudurra. Susannah cares for all of us.

Suddenly he realised they had lost sight of David. But it didn't seem to matter: Susannah paused outside a building. This one was larger than all the others. Long white marble stairs led up to tall marble pillars, and then great open wooden doors, intricately carved. Faris stared up at a gleaming rounded roof. Fat pigeons peered down at him.

'In here.' Susannah climbed the long stairs. Each one shone as though someone had scrubbed it. Faris followed through the doors, into a hall so high it echoed. It too had marble pillars and a blue-green marble floor, shining as though it had just been polished.

'What is this place?' he whispered.

'You'll see.' Susannah led the way across the hall to two closed wooden doors, carved and polished like the front door had been. She pushed. One door opened slightly. She slipped through, with Faris just behind her.

The room inside was vaster than the lecture theatre at his first school — a hundred times bigger — with tier after tier of seats, all filled with people like the ones outside: well-dressed women with hats and gloves, men in suits but with their hats in their laps. They sat in silence, staring at a wide, empty stage.

There was no sign of David.

Even a whisper would break the quiet. Susannah sat in one of two seats that were somehow vacant, the only empty seats in the whole theatre. Faris sat next to her. The lights dimmed. A spotlight shone on the stage.

The audience rose to their feet, clapping, as David's small figure crossed the vast empty stage, a violin in his hand. He no longer wore his strange short woollen suit, but black trousers, a shirt as white as morning sunlight and a white bow tie. Somehow the stage no longer looked empty, as though David's mere presence was everything it needed.

David bowed, his hair flopping down over his face, then falling back as he lifted his head again. The audience sat. Once more silence filled the theatre.

'Today's performance will begin with "Jamila's Song".' David lifted the violin and settled it under his chin. He lifted the bow and began to play.

The music was a voice, a song. It was the melody that Jamila sang back on the beach, a million times now. Its beauty was like an arrow that pierced you and held you still, so that it was only you and the music in the world. Faris could almost hear the words now: words of loss, of anguish, but something more. The music was somehow more vivid than the hall, the audience, the shops outside.

He shut his eyes and let the notes fill him. He knew little about music. There had been nothing like this since his father had been taken away, except sometimes songs on TV.

My father would love this music, he thought. His father, working at the Australian hospital …

Faris opened his eyes. For a second all he could see was grey. Grey, like the storm sea and the sky, though the music still soared around. He blinked, and the audience were there again, the high dome of the ceiling, the red carpet on the floor.

Slowly a coldness filled him, despite the beauty of the music. His skin crawled as though ants tracked across his body. He felt the tears even before he knew why they were there, felt Susannah's hand in his, clutched her, the only warmth around.

'Come on,' she whispered, under the sound of David's music.

He shook his head. It would be rude to disturb the audience, intent as they were on the music from the stage. Susannah pulled his hand. This time he obeyed her.

No one even noticed as they walked out.

The entrance hall was empty. Faris could still hear faint music; he could almost hear the silence too, from the hundreds who watched and listened. But the song's almost-words had vanished from his mind.

Faris stared at the marble pillars, at the shining floor, at the men and women walking along the footpath outside, the gleaming, old-fashioned cars purring along the clean and quiet street.

'What's happening?' he whispered. 'Where are we? I don't understand.'

'You're not alone in that, boyo. But come back to the sand hill. I'll explain it all there.' There was endless compassion in her eyes.

'You'll answer my questions?'

'Oh, yes,' said Susannah gently.

'Billy said we weren't to ask questions on the beach.'

Susannah was already walking out the door, into the street. 'The sand hill isn't the beach, remember? Billy is a good boy.' Susannah spoke as if she was forty, not ten. 'He does his best for us. But happens my idea of what is best isn't always the same as Billy's. I keep Billy's laws on the beach, and he knows it. But the sand hill is my place for talking.'

59

They could see the sand hill now, erupting strangely from the city street. Faris began to climb it with relief.

Halfway up he looked back.

The city street was gone. Kangaroos grazed under trees laden with orange blossom, between houses with shiny cars.

CHAPTER 8

They sat on the warm sand, the golden beach before them, the young people throwing the ball, Mudurra laughing as Juhi threw the ball over his head, to plop down into Nikko's waiting arms. Jamila laughed too, as though she had never sung of loss or longing.

Faris glanced behind him. His own street was still there, even though he could see David's footprints leading down to what had been a city street.

'What is this place?' he whispered. 'What's happening? Is this Australia?'

Susannah looked at him with sympathy. 'It's hard, isn't it? When someone new comes, I wait before I try to explain it. You have to find the right time, the moment each person wants to understand.'

'I want to understand,' he said roughly. 'Tell me what is happening! Does everyone except me know what's happening here?'

'I don't think Nikko understands.' Susannah smiled as she looked down at the little boy running to pick up the ball rolling along the sand. 'He's so young that he doesn't realise how strange this is. He just accepts it.'

'Accepts what?! How can there be three different lands in the same place?' Faris tried to keep the desperation from his voice.

'There's more than that. There's a different land for every one of us.'

He stared at her. It was impossible. But he had already seen the impossible. Life is impossible, he thought, swinging from safety to terror in minutes. But we manage to live it, just the same.

Susannah was already answering the question he had yet to ask. 'We just saw David's Australia. The one he imagined in a place called a concentration camp, before he came here.'

There was no need to whisper, Faris realised. The gentle whoosh of the waves stopped their words reaching the players on the beach. There was no one to hide from here.

Susannah looked at him steadily. 'The home you go back to each night is *your* Australia. The one you dreamed of.'

'No! My home isn't a dream!' Suddenly he remembered his fear on the first night, after he'd been to the beach. His bedroom, his whole new life *was* exactly what he had dreamed. Even the streets he'd wandered had been just like the Australian streets he'd imagined he'd be coming to.

But not the beach.

'I never dreamed of a beach like this!'

'Nor did I. Nor Billy. But Mudurra did.'

Faris looked down at the young man calling out something as he threw the ball to Juhi. 'The beach is Mudurra's dream?'

'I don't know,' said Susannah quietly. 'Mudurra came here first, long, long before the rest of us.

Maybe the beach has always been here, waiting for those who need it. Maybe Mudurra imagined it, just like you imagined the house you live in now. Mudurra never leaves the beach. This is all the world he has.'

'Not even at night?'

Susannah shook her head.

Faris shivered. He wanted to argue, to yell it couldn't be true. Yet Susannah had the voice of someone who wouldn't lie. Couldn't lie perhaps. She might hold back the truth till you were strong enough to hear it, but she wouldn't make things up.

'We're in Australia,' he whispered. 'We have to be!'

'How did you get to Australia then?' asked Susannah quietly.

'I ... I don't remember.' He didn't want to remember. The one thing he was certain of was that the dark place in his mind should not be lit up. 'I ... I think I had an accident on the journey here. I lost my memory. It's called amnesia ...' His words now sounded desperate, even to himself — as though using a technical term could make his words true.

Susannah gazed at him with soft sympathy in her eyes. 'But you're starting to remember.' She took his hand. Once again hers felt both small and strong. 'We all arrived here, trying so hard to forget. Every one of us had to face things that are too big for children. But I think you're ready to remember now.'

'I ... I don't want to remember,' he whispered. His cheeks were cold. Suddenly he realised tears were falling.

She held out a handkerchief — a surprisingly white one, given the drabness of her dress, and trimmed with white lace. Then to his shock she called out, 'Billy!'

'No!' protested Faris. He couldn't cry in front of Billy.

Down on the sand Billy tossed the ball to Jamila. He strode up the sand hill and flopped down next to them. 'Far Eyes remember how he got here yet?'

'No,' said Faris. He couldn't remember. Didn't want to remember.

'Yes,' said Susannah.

And suddenly it was there, his whole life. Jadda muttering with irritation as she put on her hijab to go to her job at school, the blood on the kitchen table after the police dragged his father away, the empty frightened years as he and Jadda withdrew to a nation of two inside the tiny flat. The refugee camp, the boat ...

'The wave,' he whispered. 'It was like a mountain rising out of the sea. Then it came down —' All at once he was sobbing, telling it all, from his father's white face and the blood on his jacket, the call in the night that had begun the journey here, his hands over his wet face, unable to stop.

He felt Susannah's arm around his shoulders, heard Billy's voice, surprisingly gentle. How could Billy be gentle? 'It's all right, matey. You're safe here now. Don't you fret none. You're safe.'

'Safe.' Faris took his hands away. He looked at the beach, the neat waves that slipped up the sand and back, blue waves, not black, and then behind him, at the comfortable clean street, the rose gardens and orange trees.

It had to be real! But all at once its very beauty stabbed him with grief. And Jadda, the Jadda he had left this morning. How could that Jadda not be real?

Because she is a memory, he thought, suddenly understanding why his Jadda here had dark hair, not grey.

'We understand,' said Susannah softly.

'How can you?' His voice was harsh and fierce. 'No one can understand.' He had left Jadda in the water, he realised. Vanished here, to this golden beach, leaving Jadda to the wave.

'We've been there too.'

He stared at her. 'You ... you were in a boat like I was?'

'Oh, yes.' Susannah's voice was serene. 'Bigger than yours, I'm thinking, but still a speck, a grain of sand in a vast ocean. Coming from Ireland we were, in 1923.'

1923! But Susannah kept on speaking, as though the impossible date didn't matter.

'My mam and sixteen children, and every one of us dreaming of Australia. Da was already there, with a good job and a good house for us, with glass in all the windows, he wrote to us, and all the butter we could eat. We could go to school in Australia, every one of us.

'And then I got the fever. Maybe it was typhoid, or the measles. I just remember my head screaming

65

like it was going to burst, my body hot and cold at the same time, the pain so fierce that it was red, then black. Everything was black.

'I woke up here.'

'On the beach?' She's lying, he thought. 1923 and a ship from Ireland? She had to be lying. But somehow he couldn't believe that Susannah would lie to him.

Susannah shook her head. 'No one wakes up on the beach, except Mudurra. We all wake up in our own worlds and find our way to the beach. I was in a bed. A lovely feather bed, all to myself — not six of us crammed head to toe, not the bunk we shared on the ship — just like I'd dreamed I'd have in Australia. When I go home each evening, there's Mam and Da and a pot of stew waiting on the fire, a big jug of milk that never empties, and fresh bread and all the butter we can eat every morning, for me brothers and sisters too. But they don't come down to the beach. Took me weeks to realise they weren't real ...' The anguish whispered behind the calm of her voice.

'They are real!' Billy's voice was clipped. 'Real as makes no difference! So what if your brothers and sisters can't come down here? You've got us to play the game with, ain't you?' He stared defiantly down as Mudurra tossed the ball to Jamila on the beach.

Susannah said nothing. It was the loudest nothing Faris had ever heard. He looked at Billy again. 'Did you come from Ireland too?'

Billy snorted. 'Do I sound like a bog trotter to you? Or smell like Hogan's goat? I were a convict, weren't I? But at least I'm an English one, and not no Mick.'

'But convicts were long ago.'

'You think I'm lyin'? Why would I want to lie about that? I ain't no snollygoster. If I were lyin', I'd make meself a prince, not convict scum.' He stared out at the sea. 'Not sure when we set sail, but it were about 1827, I reckon.'

1923? 1827? The dates were impossible. But Faris thought about the old cars that had looked new in David's world, the lamp in the window of Susannah's house.

Billy was still speaking, as though the words were being pulled out of him. 'Three hundred of us, I reckon, crammed down in the hold. No daylight, just dead rats washing around our bunks. One popped once, right by my head. Covered me in rat blood and bits of bone. They fed us once a day, let down buckets of stew, and biscuit if we were lucky. You grabbed what you could and if you couldn't then you starved.'

Faris stared at him in horror.

'But I'm big.' Billy drew himself up. 'I fought for my food. I fought every day. Then one day I looked around and there in the dark was Lunger McCoy with a knife he'd made by sharpening a spoon to a razor's edge. He held it to my throat ...' His voice had risen with the memory. He forced it calm again. 'He was goin' to cut my throat easy as shellin' peas, there in the dark, and no one wouldna known who did it. Wouldna cared neither. The fewer of us alive, the more food for everyone else.

'Next thing I knew, I were in a bed. A proper bed, with sheets and quilt, just like in that geezer's room

67

when we skinned down the chimney to skim his pocket watch and fob. I found the beach, and there was Mudurra, Ah Goon and the others. No more starvin'. No more coves who'd cut your throat for a crust of bread. More an' more of us came. It were all good then, every bit of it. I didn't remember nothin' about the ship, nor about bein' a convict neither,' he nodded at Susannah, 'till she came. She was the one who made us all remember.' His words were bitter now. 'Who wants to remember the bad stuff when you got all this?'

Faris felt like a wind was buffeting his brain. He'd read about convicts on the internet, when he'd looked up the history of Australia. 'But convicts were two hundred years ago!' He stared. 'How old are you?' White skin, he thought, that had felt no sun for months.

Billy lifted his chin. 'Fifteen.'

'He's been fifteen for more than a hundred years. Two hundred maybe.' Susannah's voice was calm and clear. Though Faris could still hear the echo of pain. 'I'm ten. I don't know how long I've been ten. But it's been a long time. Eighty years maybe. A terrible long time.'

'Not terrible at all! A good time,' insisted Billy. 'What's the likes of me to go back to, eh? Dying in the dark? I got seven years to serve even if I reach Botany Bay. You know what that's like at Botany Bay?'

Faris shook his head.

'Cove on the ship could read. He'd read a newspaper back home. Said as how convicts in Australia get

68

chained together, have to make roads with pickaxes, up in the mountains till they're blue with cold, till they drop with the hunger and die in their chains. If you speaks out or tries to run, you get the lash. Coves die under the whip out there. Seven years of that, an' only if I'm *lucky*,' Billy made the word a sneer, 'enough to live. You know what I got here?'

'Billy lives on a farm in his Australia,' said Susannah. 'There are horses and sheep —'

'An' they're all mine. Big fires in every room. An' roast beef every day,' said Billy. 'Grilled kidneys and kippers for breakfast, an' all the toast I want, and mutton chops for dinner and roast beef for my supper, unless I want a goose or pork pie.'

Faris remembered the meat, the heavy loaves of bread Billy had brought down to the beach, the stone jugs of apple juice. Every time he wanted to think this was impossible another piece of the jigsaw fitted in.

'And puddings and pies, I'm never hungry, not for nothin', never! And no work neither. Just playing like this, every day, on the beach.' Billy looked a challenge at Susannah. 'It's a good life.'

'But not a real one,' said Susannah quietly.

Faris felt his heart empty. 'We're dead then?'

'No, o' course not!' said Billy, just as Susannah cried, 'No!'

'I was drowning. You had the fever. Billy was going to have his throat cut —'

'How can we be dead?' said Susannah sharply. 'This isn't heaven.'

'Then what is it?'

'A refuge,' she said quietly. 'It took me years to find the answer. I sat on the sand hill. I prayed, day after day. And one day the answer came. We are the children who refused to die. Instead of dying we have come here to build up the strength to go back to what we have to face, the strength to live. The strength to go back to our lives and to survive.'

She looked at Faris, then at Billy. 'I knew something else then too. I knew it was my job to help us remember. I knew I had to stay here to help each one of us go back.'

Billy snorted. 'Why does there have to be a reason? We're here. That's all that matters. Don't you listen to her, Far Eyes. You stay here and you forget.'

Forget? How could he forget now?

Faris shut his eyes. 'My grandmother,' he whispered. 'I left her there. Abandoned her. But I didn't mean to leave her. I didn't mean to be a coward.' He opened his eyes.

'See?' said Billy. 'Remembering hurts.'

'You're not a coward,' said Susannah fiercely. She gave Billy a sharp look too. 'And neither are you.'

'What are we then?' demanded Faris.

'Brave.'

Faris remembered how he had cried on the boat, how the sea had drunk his tears. 'I'm not brave.'

'True bravery doesn't know how brave it is. I think our beach is where only the very brave come, children who have been travelling to Australia, from many times, from many places. Who've faced things impossible to face. Who come here till they can go on living.'

70

'And then what happens?' Faris whispered.

'You go back.'

Billy folded his arms in challenge. 'Or if they've got the sense, stay here.'

Faris looked across the beach, almost unable to bear its beauty. Leave? Go back to the wave? To Jadda, he told himself. 'How can I get back?' he demanded of Susannah. Then he knew.

He looked along the beach, at the tumbled rocks. 'The doorway.' That strange doorway that had called him on his second day at the beach; the door he had so carefully avoided ever since.

Susannah nodded. 'When anyone goes through that doorway, they vanish. They go back to where they came from.'

Faris stared at her. It was impossible. But everything that had happened in the last few days — even the last few years — had been impossible too.

'Has anyone ever come back?'

'No. None have returned.'

'Then how do you know where they go to? Or when?' It would be bad — impossibly bad — to go through that doorway and face the wave. It would be worse to go through and find a calm flat sea, weeks or even months after the bodies and debris had floated away.

'Because Mudurra says so. He says the door leads back to our old lives. Our real lives.'

'How does he know?'

Billy looked at him in a way Faris would once have found threatening. 'Mudurra knows this beach like

71

you know your hand. Don't you go thinkin' that 'cause Mudurra's a darkie he's less'n you nor me.'

Susannah laid her small hand on Billy's white arm. Despite all his time on the beach, the convict had not reddened or darkened in the sun.

Somewhere, sometime, Billy Higgs was still in a dark hold on a convict ship.

'Hush with you,' said Susannah to Billy. 'Mudurra has been here longer than any of us,' she continued to Faris. 'We never quite believed when he said the doorway could take us back. Then Ah Goon went through it. We'd been talking, Ah Goon and me. Suddenly he remembered what had happened to him, just like you did today. He said he was going through the doorway, to try to go back to his ship. Ah Goon had been on a ship exploring Australia, a Chinese one, long before even Billy got here.'

That didn't make sense. 'The English were the first here,' declared Faris. 'They found the Aboriginal people here.'

Billy snickered. 'You were there, were you? You know just what happened?'

'The internet says so.'

'An' who's the internet then, that he knows it all?'

'The internet is —' Faris stopped. How did you explain the internet to a fifteen-year-old from 1827? Machines talking to machines across the world? He'd think it was impossible.

As impossible as a beach and an imagined Australia where you vanished from danger ... but could go back.

'Ah Goon were here afore me, and Pedro, Jan and Henri too. They was all on ships. Pedro and Henri, they had the scurvy real bad. Their teeth was fallin' out. Jan was going to be speared by some blacks. Spears even bigger'n Mudurra's, he reckoned. Ah Goon was washed overboard, in a storm.'

'When Ah Goon stepped back through the door, we saw where he was going.' Susannah's voice was quiet with remembered horror. 'We saw the waves, saw the side of the giant black ship. Ebony, Ah Goon said it was, the blackest wood in all the world.'

'Saw him saved? Or saw him die?'

'Ah Goon lived,' declared Susannah. 'He *had* to live.'

'Except you don't know that at all,' said Billy flatly. 'Why do you think Mudurra's never gone back, eh? Who knows what really happened when Ah Goon went through the door? Maybe the poor cove drowned, or a shark ate him. Pedro, Henri and Jan went through the door after Ah Goon went. Maybe they all died too, or worse. Susannah thinks we should all be heading through that door, back to what we escaped from. But I say nuts to that. I say we're better off here, where life is good.'

'Where you'll always be fifteen,' challenged Susannah. 'Where nothing changes. All we have is what we remember, the Australia that we dreamed of.'

'And ain't that good enough? Better'n good? What if you got Ah Goon, Jan an' the others to walk through that doorway, just to find their deaths on the other side? What of that, eh?'

'They may have died,' said Susannah softly. 'But I don't think so. Death is easy for people like us, the easiest thing in our whole lives. But to survive — that's harder. I think that's why we're here. To find the strength, the courage to survive.'

'You think,' snorted Billy. 'But you don't know.'

'How many have come here?' asked Faris. 'How many have left?'

Billy glanced at Susannah. 'Show him yer book.'

Susannah reached into her apron. She handed Faris the leather-covered notebook. He opened it, looking at the painfully neat writing. It was the list he'd seen before. But this time he really looked at it. 'There are dozens of names here,' he whispered.

Billy nodded. 'There were five already here when I came: Mudurra, Ah Goon, Pedro, Jan, Henri then me. Mudurra says Ah Goon came next after him. Ah Goon had some adventures, I can tell you. Did you know there's places where they wrap up women's feet to make them small?'

He didn't wait for Faris to answer. 'Never did find out where Pedro come from. Don't think he knew neither. The sailors on the ship he were on just grabbed him from the docks when he were sellin' fish, an' he couldn't speak their lingo. All he had to eat was ship's biscuit, crumbly with weevils, an' salt fish, so much salt his lips blistered. Then his legs swelled up, and his teeth started to fall out. He went to sleep one night an' woke up here.'

'Who came after you?'

'Big Johnny came after me, then Bridget. She

were Irish, starving.' Billy shook his head. 'She were starved when she got on the ship, and starved on the way here too. Never saw no one so thin, not even David. Then Gow Lee, he were after gold, goin' to send money back to his family till his ship were wrecked; and then Wolfgang — they came only a few days apart, but Wolfgang's family were farmers, not after gold. Two ships but the same storm wrecked them both, I reckon.'

Billy glanced at Susannah. They argue about everything, but there's friendship too, thought Faris wonderingly. He remembered Billy throwing gentle balls to Nikko, and how Susannah had immediately called Billy when she saw that Faris was starting to remember. How had he never seen the friendship between them before? Both of them doing their best for the others, even if they disagreed about what 'the best' was.

'Mudurra, Pedro and the others were just muckin' about on the beach till I got here. It was me got them playin' the game,' Billy was saying, with a touch of pride. 'The game is fun. It brings us together too. All of us from different times and different places. Don't none of that matter when you play the game. Then Susannah got here.'

He shook his head. 'Soon as she remembered where she came from, she started making us remember too. Naggin' at us. "Go back,"' he imitated in a mockery of Susannah's accent. 'An' one by one they all went through the door. All me friends, gone to who knows where?'

'To their real lives,' said Susannah fiercely. 'This place gives us the strength to live.'

'For what? Months with the rats and the darkness, then seven years with a ball an' chain around me leg?' Billy shrugged. 'Well, maybe Pedro and Jan and Henri had more to go back for than me, if they managed to get to where they was goin', an' managed to live. But me? If I get to Botany Bay, I'm naught but convict scum. I'm someone here, king of the beach, boss of my farm. An' here I'm stayin'.'

Faris looked down at the players. 'What about the others?'

'Jamila will go back,' said Susannah. 'Soon, I think.'

'She'll stay here if she knows what's good for her! Every one of us is better off here,' said Billy. 'But that don't stop Susannah naggin' us to go back. Now she'll be trying to get you to go through that dashed door too.'

'Faris ...' began Susannah.

Suddenly Faris felt the same anger as Billy. How dare this small girl ask him about things that hurt, force him to remember? How dare she expect him to go back, to leave the beach and its sunlight, Jadda and the big clean house with its books and computer?

'Then why don't you go through the door yourself?' he demanded.

'Because if I go, there'll be no one to remind you all of what you've left behind.' She gazed down at the small group, still playing ball on the sand. 'When I got here, they'd all forgotten there could be anything but this beach and the homes they go to at night.'

She met Faris's eyes. He shifted uncomfortably, still unused to a girl's direct gaze. 'But they're dream homes, just like this is a dream beach. And one day everyone here needs to go back to what's real, no matter how hard it is.'

'You believe that?'

'I do.'

'An' I don't,' said Billy. He glared across the sand at the doorway, as if he wished the next tide would wash it away. But it looked too secure for that, jammed between its rocks. 'All of us here now, we've decided to stay here. An' you will too, if you've got sense. An' you'll keep my rules, down on the beach. No questions, no memories. An' if you go to someone else's home, you don't ask no questions about the past there neither. No questions, no tryin' to make us remember. Never.'

'Except on the sand hill,' said Susannah.

Billy shrugged, as if the scrubby sand hill could never compete with the beach of golden sand. 'So, are you staying?'

Faris thought of the black wave, of Jadda waiting for him back in the house, the bright fresh house that seemed so real. And maybe tomorrow he would try the new computer. Maybe tomorrow his father would be back from the hospital ...

What had he to return to, except terror and almost certain death?

'I'll stay,' he said. But his eyes still shifted to the rough timber doorframe among the rocks.

CHAPTER 9

The computer stared at him when he woke the next morning, its gleaming flat screen just like the advertisements he had seen. He remembered where he had seen a computer like this now — in the in-flight magazine when they had flown to Indonesia. He had longed to try one.

Now he could. All he had to do was turn it on.

Nothing changes here. He heard Susannah's words again. He had never turned on this model computer. He never would, not if he stayed here.

Now he knew why his father was always at the hospital. For he had no father, not one he knew. The man who had been taken, the man who would have swallowed his scream as the police wrenched his arm, he knew that man was gone.

He still had a father, somewhere. But that man had gone through years of prison, torture, if even a fraction of the rumours were true. The man in Australia was Faris's father, but not the one he knew.

There was no father for him here.

But there was Jadda. He got up, dressed, in jeans again but a different-coloured T-shirt, went out to find the buffet breakfast, the one on the holiday websites for the place called Uluru and for the Great Barrier

Reef. Those are from my memories, he thought. This is my version of Australia. No wonder the food had little taste. He had seen it in photos of Australian resorts on the internet: he had never actually tasted it. Only imagined. Only dreamed.

But he had known Jadda. Did know her. He hugged her especially hard this morning, heard her laugh as she hugged back, smelled her hand cream.

If this is memory and imagination, he thought, as he sat down to drink the tall glass of pineapple juice, topped with an umbrella and a cherry, then it's good. Just like Billy said.

But it was different now. He knew it. He couldn't let it go.

He looked around the room. There would never be a surprise in this room, never something new to find.

He looked up to find Jadda watching him. 'Go to the beach,' she said softly. 'Go and be with your friends.'

It was what Jadda would have said. It was what he knew he needed too.

He hugged her hard again, swiftly. Even if she was from his memory, she was still the Jadda he loved, who loved him too.

He jogged along the quiet street. No children played in the gardens. No women walked the footpath with shopping baskets. No one drove the shiny cars.

Why hadn't he seen it before?

Because I didn't want to, he thought. Because I needed quiet and safety.

He climbed the sand hill. Down on the beach Billy, Susannah, Mudurra and Juhi tossed the ball to each other. Billy hadn't mentioned Juhi, he realised. She must have come with Mudurra. But then Juhi was only a girl. He trudged down the sand. Billy looked up at him and gave a grin of relief.

'Hey, good to see you, matey. Come on down.'

He's glad I haven't gone through the doorway, thought Faris. He's glad I'm still here, and safe. Billy wasn't the bully he had at first thought. He was a protector, just like Susannah.

One by one the others wandered down the sand hill and joined in the game. Faris looked at them curiously. It was as though until now they had just been playmates, part of the game. Now he suddenly wanted to know their stories and who they were.

Susannah brought down a mutton-and-potato stew for lunch. It wasn't spiced like Jamila's, but it was fatty and comforting. Did your mother make the stew? thought Faris, as he ran up the beach and took the giant pot from her. Or did it just appear, like my giant buffet breakfast is always on the table when I come out from the bathroom?

Where had Jamila come from? What was her dream Australia like? Were her bright scarves and dresses from her past, or were they the clothes she had longed for?

The stew had little bones in it, but it was good. Faris ate two servings. It's new, he told himself. There were new things to discover on the beach, if not in his house. Perhaps he could visit the memories and dreams of all his friends. They would be new too.

Billy sopped chunks of soft white bread in the stew.

He ate with both hands; he slurped and gnawed the bones. Mudurra sipped from his bowl, wrinkled his nose, then wandered back along the beach. Juhi ate hers quickly, smiled an apology and followed him.

Susannah picked up a bone in her fingers and began to chew the meat more neatly than Billy. Faris thought of going down into that small cottage, with its smell of cows. He'd never seen a land so green. What would it be like to go through that cottage door? His friends could visit him and Jadda too ...

No! He didn't want anyone to come to his world now. It would remind him that it was a dream. Dreams are private things, he thought. That's why we meet here on the beach, share our food and laughter but nothing else. David's dreams were different — he needed an audience, a real one, not just the one that he imagined.

He looked at the others, still silently eating. Somehow he knew that even if they had seen each other's worlds, they didn't do it often. It was hard enough keeping their own Australias real without adding guests. He shook his head. He felt confused, bruised by too much to understand.

The game began again. The waves sang. Small waves. Safe waves. A wind eddied along the beach. Susannah walked up and sat on the sand hill.

Faris tried to focus on the ball. Billy is right, he thought. It hurt to ask questions, here on the glowing beach. It hurt if you thought too much. He should just enjoy it, the happiness, the safety.

But his brain kept working, as if it was a computer, as if it had been programmed to keep thinking.

He didn't want to play today, he realised. He'd go back to his house, to Jadda. This time he *would* turn on the computer. If a buffet breakfast could feel real, then so would the computer. He might never have used that model before, but he had read about it, could imagine it.

He stepped away, then began a slow walk up the damp sand, packed hard by the waves, then onto the hot dry sand. He had never left the beach so early before.

'Far Eyes!'

He turned. It was Mudurra, striding up the beach towards him. A giant fish hung across his shoulders, its mouth gaping, its eyes staring.

Mudurra grinned. 'You want a fish?' He thrust the fish at him.

Faris took it automatically. It felt cool and surprisingly heavy. 'Thank you.'

Was the gift a way of making Faris welcome on the beach, keeping him happy so he wouldn't go through the door? Faris imagined Jadda's expression when he arrived with a giant fish in his arms. 'King Faris of the computers has decided to be a cook, has he? Or do the marketing?' He shook his head. Jadda felt real. *Was* real, even if she was made of memory. Memory was real too. 'It's very kind of you,' he added to Mudurra.

Mudurra raised one shoulder in what might be a kind of shrug. 'There are fish. I catch them.'

Day after day, thought Faris. Century after century, if Susannah was right. 'My name is Faris. Not Far Eyes.'

'Faris.' Mudurra tried out the word.

Faris nodded. 'You speak good English.'

'English?'

'English. The language.'

Mudurra gave another of his almost-shrugs. 'I speak what I speak.'

Faris had thought everyone spoke English on the beach. English was the language of Australia. But Mudurra had come here before English even existed. Ah Goon could not have known English either. Somehow he didn't see Billy giving everyone lessons. Another of the beach's mysteries, he thought. Whatever language we speak here is the same for all of us. 'Does Mudurra mean anything?' he asked cautiously.

'Mudurra.'

Mudurra grinned at Faris's reaction. He pantomimed a bird, a giant one, balanced on the wind.

'You are named after a bird?'

'A bird that flies a long way. Like me.'

Faris let himself feel curious. Who was this young man who had had the strength to live with only himself for so long? Though he must have had Juhi for company too.

'Is Juhi your sister?'

Mudurra looked startled. 'Juhi came here just before you.'

Faris stared at him. 'She's from modern times? But she doesn't wear proper clothes.'

'Her fur is good fur. Soft, well cured.' Mudurra sounded amused, as though clothes were not important. Faris supposed they weren't, for a young man who wore only string and a knife. 'But she is not from the same place or time as me.'

Faris wondered where modern girls still wore scraps of fur. 'Where do *you* come from then?'

He almost expected Mudurra to say that he had always been there. Instead Mudurra said, 'I come from two arms from where the sun rises in the sea.'

Faris tried to work it out. 'North?'

'Ah Goon called it the north.' Mudurra shrugged. 'North is a word. The sun and moon and stars are there in the sky.'

'When did you come?'

Mudurra seemed to find that funny too. 'In the season of flowering, two flowerings after the year the great whale beached beyond the headland. Ah Goon measured the seasons one way, Susannah and Jamila in another.' Mudurra gestured at the arched blue sky, the flat blue sea. 'What does it matter? The days pass here. The seasons. As many seasons as there are stars in the sky.'

Faris hesitated. 'How did you get here?'

He knew the question would hurt. Or would it, after so long? Did pain slowly vanish, here in their refuge?

Mudurra stared out at the sea. He was silent so long that Faris thought he wasn't going to answer. At last he said, 'The mountain shivered near our camp. The sky burned. Rocks fell and then the ash. We ran for the canoes ...'

A volcano! For a moment Faris felt superior. He knew what a volcano was and what made it erupt, while this young man did not. But Mudurra had known a real volcano, in all its savagery and terror. His pride vanished. 'And then?'

Mudurra laughed again. It was a laugh that said, 'Laughter is better than crying with fear.'

'We paddled through the ash, as the sea turned to blood like the sky. We paddled towards the great track of stars that arrow through the sky, but we could not see them, because of the ash. Great-Uncle said, "Dream of the land across the sea, the land where the white smoke rises in the season of no rain." The ash fell and the sea sizzled. I dreamed that a beach of sand waited for us. Clean sand, with no falling ash, with a sky that was blue, not red.' He shrugged. 'Then I was here.'

'Alone?'

The young man nodded. 'I was alone for a long time. I walked the beach, me and the waves and the sand. I speared fish, big ones, small ones. I ate them. I slept on the warm sand. There is fresh water if you dig for it, under the sand hill. I watched the great white sweep of stars. Sometimes I thought I dreamed this place, just like Great-Uncle said to do. I dreamed of going back. When I woke the door was there, propped in the sand. I knew if I stepped through it, I would be back with the boiling sea. How could I go back to that? I dreamed of friends. Then Ah Goon came, and then the others. It was better then.'

Faris stared at him. How long had Mudurra been alone here? Hundreds of years? Or thousands? Maybe, he thought, time doesn't work the same here.

He looked at the darkness of Mudurra's eyes. Even if time was not quite the same, this was the face of someone who had known a world with only one pair of footprints on the sand.

No wonder Mudurra doesn't always play the game with us, he thought. We must be like ants to him, scurrying in tiny sand lives, instead of the long hard rock of his.

Had Mudurra's canoe been the first to head to Australia?

Had Mudurra really dreamed up this beach? Had he dreamed up the doorway too, so that each could leave, so that no one would be stranded here forever?

'Did you ever try to leave? Not through the door,' Faris added hurriedly, trying not to look at the two big hunks of driftwood with the tattered skin hanging between them. 'Didn't you try to find other people?'

'Yes. I thought at first I had been washed onto a safe beach, on a new land. I walked across the sand hill.'

Mudurra was silent suddenly.

'What did you see?' asked Faris cautiously.

The dark eyes gazed out to sea. 'Another sand hill. I walked up it — and there was this beach below.' He looked Faris in the eyes. Mudurra rarely looked directly at anyone, but when he did you felt his gaze. 'Ah Goon tried to walk beyond the world he'd dreamed. He came back to where he'd left, no matter which way he went.' Mudurra's voice was grim. 'You've remembered how you came here, haven't you?'

Faris nodded.

'Do not try to leave by walking.'

Faris thought of the time he'd spent wandering the streets of houses, green lawns and grazing kangaroos. He shivered. 'I won't.'

'I thought that maybe the others had been washed onto a beach nearby and I could find them.' Mudurra gestured at the cliffs on either side of them. 'You cannot climb the cliffs. Even with ropes. Time after time I tried. I tried to swim around them too, but the waves pushed me back.

'I made a raft from driftwood on the beach. A raft to take me to another beach, and people.'

Mudurra looked out at the sea. It was impossible to read his face now. 'The water looks gentle. But it's not. When you are as far out as a man can throw a spear, a current grabs you. It is like teeth that won't let go.'

Mudurra gestured to the line of giant rocks across the mouth of the bay. 'The current tried to dash my raft against the cliffs. I dived off. The current took me. It tried to smash me against the rocks. At last I got free and swam back to the beach. I lay on the sand with no strength all through the night and day, too weak even to get water.' He looked straight at Faris. 'I have tried to leave five times. The sixth time the current will kill me. I will not try to leave that way again.'

Faris tried not to imagine Mudurra's body, helpless, lying exhausted on the empty beach. He stared out at the tall black rocks across the bay. They looked like prison bars now. 'The only way to leave is through the door,' said Mudurra. 'The only place to go to is the one that you have left.'

You could escape into memory and imagination, thought Faris. But neither led you anywhere, except in the real world. In the real world imagination and hard work might lead you to become a software engineer, a physicist, an astronomer.

But there was no way into the real world unless you stepped back, into the danger that lay through the doorway. The beach was their prison, as well as their refuge. The only way out was back to what you had left.

Mudurra was still gazing at the black rocks across the bay. Faris said quickly, to change the subject, 'I think Juhi likes you.'

Mudurra glanced back at Juhi as she danced forwards two steps to throw the ball to Jamila. His face softened for a moment, then became carefully blank once more. He gave a laugh, a bark of bitterness, not humour. 'I cannot have a wife till I am a man. I have told Juhi, but she will not hear.' He looked down at the young woman again. 'I will never be a man here.'

'You mean because you can't grow older?'

Mudurra looked back at Faris. 'Why would I want to grow older, for my bones to ache, to no longer be able to cast a spear so far? I am happy to be as I am. But you must be a warrior to take a wife, and you must learn things to be a warrior. There is no other man here, no warriors, to make me a warrior too. A stranger would not understand.'

'I think I do. A bit. I ... I'm scared to go through the doorway too.'

'A warrior is never scared,' said Mudurra flatly.

But you're not a warrior. You are a young man, playing on the beach and spearing fish. Faris would not say the words, but they hung in the salt air around them nonetheless.

'You think I am a coward? You think I should go back to the world where air is ash and sky is blood? I dreamed of a new land, as Great-Uncle said. A good land. You think I should leave it now?'

'I don't think you are a coward.'

'Then you are a fool. I am a coward. I should step through the door for a chance to become a warrior so I can say to a girl like Juhi, "Come with me and be my wife." I should go back and face the falling rocks, the burning sky. But the days pass. Night after night I watch the great path of stars travel across the sky. Day after day I watch a beautiful girl upon the beach. And I am a coward still.'

And suddenly Mudurra was gone, jogging down the sand hill onto the beach. He waded out into the water, then dived down.

For a moment Faris wondered if he was going to try to swim beyond the bay again, prove he wasn't a coward. He held his breath.

But Mudurra waited for a wave, then let it bring him back to shore. A gentle wave, thought Faris. This world was gentle, safe, as Susannah had said. As long as you obeyed its rules. As long as you wanted nothing more than it could give.

'What did Mudurra say to you?' Faris hadn't noticed Juhi come up beside him.

'How he came here.'

Juhi nodded, her gaze on the young man in the waves. Suddenly Faris realised her face was trickled with tears. 'He talks to you. He won't talk to me.'

'But you're with him all the time!'

'He talks about nothing things. Fish. If the fire needs more wood.' She tore her gaze away from Mudurra. 'I'm going home.' Juhi's voice was bitter. 'Every evening he insists I walk up the sand hill, down into my world.' She shrugged. 'I could refuse. But he doesn't want me to stay on the beach with him at night.'

'He's taking care of your reputation.'

'What does it matter? We are the only ones really here! Does it matter to you, or to Susannah?' She hesitated. 'I ... I'm scared of the beach at night. I've never slept outside. I'm scared of the dark too. No streetlights. Not even a torch. But I wouldn't be scared if I was with Mudurra.'

'You come from a modern city then?'

'Of course.'

'Why don't you wear clothes?'

Juhi rubbed her hand across her tears and tried to smile. 'I do.'

'Proper clothes.'

'You mean my school uniform?'

'You went to school?' How could a girl who wore bits of fur have gone to school?

'You think I'm a savage because I have black skin and wear fur?'

It sounded insulting when she said it like that. But it was what he'd been thinking. Faris nodded.

'I think my time is pretty close to yours,' said Juhi slowly. 'I come from Sudan. Khartoum.' She lifted her chin. 'I went to the best school in Khartoum. I was the best student at my school. That was in 2003,' she added.

It was as though he had never seen her before. And I haven't, he thought. I never really looked at Juhi, and not because I was embarrassed by her bare skin. I have been too closed up inside myself to see anyone.

'You came here in 2003?' Suddenly he needed to know who she was, why a modern girl wore furs.

'No. Later. But I lost track of time when we had to leave. Lost everything.' He could hear the effort it took to keep her voice steady now.

'How are you here?' And going almost naked, he thought.

'My family is from south Sudan, but we lived in the north. My father was an engineer. But he spoke too loudly about how the people of the south were being killed, how we should fight back. We had to leave fast, into Ethiopia, to a refugee camp there. My father said that we would not have to stay in the camp long. They need engineers in Australia. He would apply to go there. Soon we would all be in Australia and safe. But the refugee camp was bad. It was run by the People's Liberation Army. They took my brother for the army. My father too.' Her voice was flat now, like Mudurra's had been, as though she was reciting a poem she had no interest in.

'What happened to you?'

'The soldiers came one night for the women. My mother heard the screaming. Where can you hide in a camp? My mother pulled our tent down, like it had collapsed. We hid under it. They saw my mother first. They pulled her out. She screamed and screamed.'

'Juhi ... Juhi, I am sorry.'

She gave a small shrug. 'I thought, I have to help her. Then I thought, I can't fight soldiers. If I move, they will find my sister too.

'I held my sister still. A hand reached in. They grabbed her leg. They pulled her out. She called, "Juhi! Juhi!" as they dragged her away. But I stayed hidden.

'I crept out when the screaming was silent, with no voices of the men. I looked for my mother, my sister. The soldiers had taken them.' Her voice was strangled as she added, 'Or they were dead. I tiptoed from tent to tent, then out into the desert in the darkness. I stumbled on till it was day. I saw women carrying water. "Help me," I said. "Please help me." But they wouldn't look at me. They pretended I wasn't there.' Tears wound down Juhi's cheeks again. How could Susannah make her remember this? thought Faris. How can I?

'Why wouldn't they help you?'

'Because I was a stranger. Those women thought, a girl who is running has enemies. We cannot save her. We will only put our families in danger.' She gave the smallest of shrugs. 'Why should they help me? I didn't help my mother, or my sister. I lay there and saved myself.'

'But you couldn't have saved them!'

'I know. That does not make it hurt less.

'I followed the women to their village, trailing behind. I went from hut to hut, begging for food, for

92

water. A boy threw a stone at me. Other boys joined in. I ran into the desert, as the boys laughed and threw stones. No one would help! Do you understand? Not the girls I thought had been my schoolfriends, not our neighbours, not the people in the camp, or these villagers. I ran again. I found another village. This one was empty.'

'What ... what had happened to the people?'

'They were there. They were dead.'

Her voice was emotionless now. 'Animals came that night, to eat the bodies. I hid in a hut. I pushed a bed against the door and one against the window. I heard them tear at bones and flesh. The morning came. I thought, I am safe now. The animals have fed. But then I heard the Jeep.' She looked at her hands. 'The army had come back. I heard them go from hut to hut, looking for weapons, for food, for women. They would see me if I ran. I pulled the bed onto its side, to hide behind it. I shut my eyes. I tried to send myself back in time, beyond the war, beyond the hatred. Then I heard footsteps in my hut. A hand grabbed my hair.'

She looked at Faris, her eyes suddenly hard. 'The soldier was your age. A boy, but smaller than you. His gun was almost as tall as him. He could have been a boy from school, grinning when he got a good mark in maths. But he grinned because he had found me.

'I thought of my mother, my sister. I kicked him and bit his arm. He yelled and then I ran. I ran out of the hut, out of the village. I ran and ran. I felt the pain before I heard the shot. The shot knocked me down. I tried to stand. I tried to call. The footsteps came closer, and closer still. My leg bled onto the sand. I had to keep going, but my eyes began to close. I thought, let me wake up ten thousand years ago. A hundred thousand!'

'You wanted to go that far to be safe?'

'I wanted to go back to the beginning! Before hatred, before people killed each other for their religion or the colour of their skin. The modern world is cruel! At school the girls laughed at me for being from the south. "No brains," they said, "they all fall out down south." My teachers did not like a girl from south Sudan being top of the class. Even my friends were not true friends.'

She stopped speaking. Faris could hear the gentle *shush* of waves, a triumphant yell as David grabbed the ball before Billy.

'I woke up in another hut,' said Juhi at last. 'A hut made of mud, soft furs for a bed. The walls glowed just a little, to keep away the dark. Outside, every tree is hung with fruit, with vines and melons. I pull at a stalk and up come sweet potatoes. Beside my hut is a fire that never goes out, even if I put no wood on it. There is an oven on it. When I open the oven door, there is fresh bread or pots of stew.'

'It sounds ...' Faris hunted for a word. 'Lovely.' No computers, he thought. Not even books or TV.

'Too lovely! It's a stupid world! A little girl's world, where food appears in an oven. But I don't know enough to make it real.' She looked down at Mudurra with a mixture of love and ferocity. 'And then I met Mudurra. His time must be close to the beginning.

94

I learned that here on the beach we can go back to different times. I thought, I can go back with him. Go back to a time before soldiers and guns.'

'I thought we only went back to our own time.'

'No one has ever tried to go with someone else!' cried Juhi. 'Don't you see?! We can go into each other's dream worlds. Why can't we share each other's pasts too?'

'You'd give up everything?' Faris tried to think of what made modern life good. 'Computers and cars and medicines, just to be safe in the past?'

'No! I am not a fool! I was top of my class! I know there has never been a time when women were truly safe. I know Mudurra's world has danger too. But maybe back there we can change the past. If we change the past enough, we can change the future too. There are too many people in the modern world, too many nations, religions, languages. No one person can make a real difference now. But back in the past there are only a few humans.' She gazed at him with fire in her eyes. 'I can make them change! Do you know the saying "God will not change a people, until they change themselves"?'

Faris nodded.

'Well, I will change them. I would change all of us.'

'With Mudurra?'

Juhi's face softened. 'He is good. Kind to all of us, even Billy. I don't know what Mudurra was like when he first came here. But he has lived for so long with people from different times and worlds. He says that some of the people who came here laughed at him at first because his skin was black. Others wouldn't play the game because girls played too, or children who had a different religion. Mudurra says that if you are kind, if you wait till the hatred wears out, all play together here. He and I could change the world together.'

Faris had never met anyone who thought they could change all of humanity, not just small bits. 'You like him,' he said at last. He wanted to say 'love'. But that would be embarrassing.

'Yes,' said Juhi softly. 'Sometimes I think he likes me too. He's taught me how to find shellfish and tend a fire. He gave me the furs.' She touched her clothes. 'They are the softest furs I have ever felt. I threw away my dress. Threw it into the sea and watched it float away.' She shook her head. 'For days I was scared it would wash up again. But it's truly gone.

'I don't want to be the person who wore those clothes. I want to go back to the bright beginning of the world. Mudurra's world.' She wrapped her thin arms around herself. 'But Mudurra never even touches me.'

'He said you were beautiful,' said Faris.

Juhi's eyes were painfully eager. 'Did he?'

'He ... he said he couldn't marry until he is a warrior, but that he needs other men to make him one. I think that's what he meant.'

'He's a warrior now,' said Juhi flatly.

'Not to himself,' said Faris softly.

Juhi stood. 'One day he'll take my hand, and we'll go back.' She strode up the sand hill on bare feet that looked as though they had never seen shoes, especially not neat school ones.

For a moment the sand seemed to blow around her. Then she was gone.

The sun hovered just above the sand hill. Soon everyone would leave the beach. Faris looked down at the fish. He picked it up and walked further up the slope to where Susannah had watched it all.

'Good night, Faris,' she said quietly.

She can guess what we were talking about, he thought. Susannah knows everything. He smiled. Susannah might not know how to write very well, but she knew love and care and friendship.

'Good night,' he replied.

Susannah smiled. 'May angels watch your rest.'

Faris nodded uncomfortably. Susannah's angels wouldn't be his. He carried the fish down the hill, then put on his shoes.

Once he would have felt embarrassed, carrying a big fish through the streets like a pedlar. But no one would laugh at him here.

For a moment he almost wished someone would come out of a house and laugh, someone new, someone he hadn't imagined or remembered. But there were only the kangaroos, peacefully tearing at the grass, and a koala snoozing in an orange tree.

He walked up the path to his front door. Jadda opened it before he could reach for the handle. She looked at his sandy hands, at the giant sandy fish, and laughed.

'King Faris of the computers has decided to be a cook, has he? Or do the marketing?' She put her book down, the one about Jane Austen in Australia, and took the fish from him. 'Good afternoon, Sir Fish,' she added. 'You are handsome, but you will look better with almonds and pomegranate sauce.'

Faris nodded. He followed her in and closed the door.

CHAPTER 10

Faris paused on top of the sand hill the next morning, just as he had on his first morning there. They had all been strangers then. Then they had become friends, the people he spent his days with. Even Billy was almost a friend. Everyone was here already today, except for little Nikko.

Suddenly Faris wanted to know Jamila's story too, and little Nikko's. The things they had seen might be terrifying, but they were fascinating too: other places, other times.

He walked down the sand hill onto the beach just as Nikko came running down behind him. 'Billy! Susannah! It is a feast today! The Feast of St Kangarou! You must all come!'

For once Susannah looked startled. 'Who is St Kangarou?'

Nikko bounced impatiently. 'St Kangarou is the patron saint of Australia! It is his feast day!' He grabbed Jamila's hand and began to drag her, laughing, up the sand hill. David followed them.

Faris looked at Susannah and Billy. 'Can we go to Nikko's world, just like we went to David's?'

'If we want,' said Susannah slowly. 'If we follow him, or if we know what it looks like.'

'That's why you sit on the sand hill? So you can know all our worlds?'

She didn't answer his question. 'Come on. This is important to Nikko.'

Faris and Susannah and Billy began to walk after the others. 'How did Nikko get here?'

'His father came to Australia to work on something called the Snowy Mountains, though maybe that isn't right. There can't be snow in Australia. It's too hot.' Susannah shrugged. 'Nikko is young. There is a lot he doesn't understand. He and his mam took a ferry to a place called Piraeus. Have you heard of it maybe?'

Faris shook his head.

'Me neither,' said Billy.

'Nikko and his mother would get a ship there,' Susannah continued. 'They'd join Nikko's father in Australia. Nikko says they had everything they owned in sacks, their clothes, his mother's candlesticks, dried bread and dried figs to eat on the voyage, even a rooster in a bag.

'Nikko let the rooster out. It perched on the ferry railing and he tried to grab it. But the sea was rough. As he climbed up onto the rail, the ferry lurched. He fell into the waves.' She looked up at the small boy, leaping over the sand hill. 'He woke up here.'

Faris looked back. Mudurra still strode among the waves with his fishing spear. Juhi glanced up at them from the sand.

'Come on!' he yelled.

Juhi shook her head. She turned back to watch Mudurra.

'Juhi won't come,' said Susannah softly. 'She doesn't want to see a modern world, even Nikko's. She'll only come if Mudurra comes too.'

'And he never leaves the beach,' said Billy.

They had reached the top of the sand hill now. Faris looked down at Nikko's world, then up.

Because somehow the land behind the sand hill rose into a mountain now. Small white houses clung to its slopes, while up above cliffs shone silver, topped with green trees. A few white shapes moved, maybe sheep, or goats.

He shook his head, in amazement and delight. A few steps and here was a new world.

A bell began to call. *Dong! Dong! Dong!* Men's voices sang above them, with the stamp of dancing feet and the strum of music. Faris sniffed. Roast lamb!

The cobbled street in front of them was empty, except for Nikko.

'Come on!' he yelled again.

Faris and Billy and Susannah followed, up the road towards the singing.

The road opened onto a big square edged by the white houses. A vast green tree shaded a well and a stone trough and tables. Whole sheep turned on spits over smouldering fires. Fat snapped and dripped onto the flames. Faris smelled rosemary and fresh bread.

All at once he heard the stamp of feet again. He gazed across the square. Men danced in a vast circle on the cobbles, hand in hand; giant men, taller than any Faris had ever seen, twice as tall as even

Mudurra. Each one had black hair and olive skin, and strong white teeth that flashed as they laughed.

Nikko skipped towards the dancers, clapping his hands, then ran back to Susannah and Billy and Faris. 'These are my uncles!' he cried. 'One day I will be as tall as them! I will dance too! My mother says so!'

'Where is your mother now?' asked Susannah.

'She is bringing the bread and cakes from the baker. My mother does not have to work here in Australia!' said Nikko proudly. 'Not even grind the grain! There is water in every house here. The cisterns never run dry! Meat every day! And today the feast!'

He scampered off as David and Jamila walked back to join them.

'Who is St Kangarou?' asked David softly. 'I've never heard of him.'

'I think we are about to find out,' said Susannah.

The music stopped. The dancing men moved to stand reverently on each side of the square.

A small procession wandered up the hill between the watching crowd. At its front two men in embroidered black-and-silver robes carried a tall gold statue standing in a long narrow box of shining wood. Behind them walked women in black dresses and black scarves and shawls. The women were normal-sized, not massive like the dancing men.

Faris stared at the statue. It looked like a man, but there was something strange about it too.

He looked again and saw the tail and paws. He stifled a giggle, saw the others were trying not to laugh too.

'St Kangarou!' whispered Susannah. 'Oh, the poor dear lad. It's all he remembers, maybe, that there are saints and saint's day feasts. So he made up St Kangarou.'

It's blasphemy, thought Faris. Blasphemy for all of them, in each of their religions. For there was no St Kangarou. There is no God but God.

But no one here prays to St Kangarou, he thought. This is a feast. Nikko doesn't even know what the word 'saint' means. It is just a feast in honour of a kangaroo. Or kangarou.

He looked at the faces of the others. Billy was enjoying it all. Faris doubted that the convict boy even knew what religion was, though he might have picked the pockets of churchgoers. Susannah, Jamila and David had expressions that were probably like his own: grins at the silly almost-human kangaroo, and doubt at what they should feel about it.

'What do we do now?' asked Faris, as the procession passed by, up through the square, then vanished into the streets above, towards the chanting bell.

'Eat,' said Billy. He nodded at the roasting sheep. Nikko was already over there, munching at a hunk of meat-filled bread. 'Smells good. Cakes and bread on the tables over there,' he added. 'What's in them baskets?'

'Apricots,' said Jamila.

'Ain't never eaten apricots before. Seen 'em at the market though.' He wandered off as the music began to play again.

Nikko darted back. 'It is good, isn't it?' He took Susannah's hand. 'Come with me. My uncles will give you the best cuts of lamb. I have told them you are my friend. You are all my friends, from the beach. Eat as much as you want today! Did you make a wish?' he added to Susannah. 'You must always make a wish when St Kangarou passes.'

'What did you wish for, Nikko?' asked Susannah softly.

'To be tall like my uncles. To dance with the men. Now come and eat!' He pulled Susannah over to the roasting lamb.

Suddenly Faris felt like crying for a small boy's happiness for an imaginary feast.

But it was real too, he reminded himself. If he ate a slice of lamb, he'd taste it. He could dance to this music too, try the pastries, the grapes and the breads.

Yet none of it would fatten him, or change the thinness of David's arms. Nor would Nikko ever grow tall like his uncles. Nikko would never dance with the men if he stayed here.

'Come on,' said Jamila softly. 'Come and feast.'

It was mid-afternoon when they got back to the beach. Nikko had stayed behind, dancing in and out of the crowd of great tall men and black-clad women, his face greasy with lamb fat, his fingers sticky from almond cakes and melon jam.

Down on the sand Mudurra and Juhi tossed the ball between them. The waves rippled back and forth.

Faris remembered something from an essay he had written on the tides. Tides were caused by the moon, the world's water swelling up, pulled by the moon's gravity. That was why tides came at slightly different times, every day, low tide, high tide ...

Except here. Every morning a high tide had washed their footprints away. But the tide never rose during the game; the waves never retreated, leaving more wet sand bare.

David lingered as the others walked down to join Juhi and Mudurra. Faris turned back to watch him.

'You're going to your world now?'

David nodded. 'You were in the audience the other day,' he added.

Faris nodded. 'Your playing is beautiful.'

'You like music?'

'I ... I think so. I haven't heard much. Not like yours.'

'Would you like to come to my concert again? Now?'

'Yes.' Faris hesitated. 'Will I still be able to find my way back home if I stay out till it gets dark?'

'The streets in my world are lighted,' said David. 'You can easily find your way back to the sand hill. Your ... home ... has streetlights too?'

'Yes.'

'Come on then. We can have Victoria sponge in a café after the concert. It is a very light cake with jam and cream. An Australian cake. We can have hot chocolate too.'

'I don't have money for a café.'

'You don't need money.' He gave a brief smile. 'Not in my Australia.'

'Could we go to your home instead?'

'No.'

Faris was shocked by the flatness of the word. 'Why not?'

'I only go there when it's late. It is my aunt's house. She lives in Australia. I have never seen her.' David shrugged. 'I never thought of her much, so perhaps I won't ever see her now, or much of her house either. Only a door, a corridor, my bed and bathroom. I just go to bed. It's a soft clean bed. The sheets are always crisp. The bathroom smells of peppermint, like no one has ever been there except me. Then I go to a café for my breakfast.' He smiled slightly. 'Big cups of hot chocolate and pastry with jam.'

It sounded like the loneliest life Faris had ever heard of. But David had his friends at the beach, he reminded himself, and the audience for his music.

'What about your family? Your parents?'

'They are dead. My mother, my father, my grandparents, my uncles and my cousins. Twenty-six of us sat at the table before the war. Now the war is over and there is only me, and an aunt I cannot even imagine in Australia.

'Are you coming to my concert?'

'Yes.'

David turned to go.

'David?' Faris needed to say this now, here on the sand hill. Somehow he knew that even in the café, eating the Australian Victoria sponge, they would be trapped in the illusion, unable to talk about their past.

'What?'

'Why don't you go back to your world? You say

106

the war is over in your time. You survived! You are a brilliant violinist, even I can tell that.'

'Yes,' said David. 'I was brilliant.' He looked down at his hands. 'I was in a place called Auschwitz. The soldiers rescued us, but I was sick. Or maybe starving. Maybe both.'

'But you've been rescued. You'll get better.'

'It doesn't matter if I get better or not.'

'I don't understand.'

'We had to work in the camp. Even us children. We worked in the snow, we slept on bare boards. Do you know what chilblains are? My hands swelled, grew red and wept. I might get better,' said David, and his voice held a world of loss. 'But my hands never will. Not enough to play the violin. Not as it should be played.' He added simply, 'I don't want to live without my music. Are you coming?'

Faris nodded. He wanted to weep, but what use were tears for David?

The two boys walked side by side through the crowded streets. Once again no one stared at Faris's jeans. David slipped into a lane at the side of the theatre and went in by the stage door. Faris continued round the front, through the auditorium and into the back seat where he had sat before. He waited for the light to shine on the stage, for David to enter, seeming to shine brighter than the light.

David lifted the violin and began to play. It was the melody he had called 'Jamila's Song' again. Had Jamila composed it? wondered Faris. But David was the musician, not her. What was Jamila's story?

The music sang across the theatre, David's fingers firm and sure. It sang of loss, but of strength too. For the first time since he had seen the beach, Faris suddenly knew that this was worth keeping, that this beauty, the knowledge of creating beauty, should not be lost.

Faris felt the tears cold on his cheeks.

David, at least, should stay here.

CHAPTER 11

Time vanished. There were no more holy days or feast days. No one ever fasted here on the beach. The days changed little, other than that one feast for St Kangarou.

Billy brought down a thick pastry filled with meat and vegetables that he said was called a pasty. Jamila brought apricots for Billy, small and with red freckles, as sweet as sunlight. Juhi brought down a big basket of fat red fruit, juicy and strange-scented, but shrugged when they asked her what they were. She rolled a giant watermelon down the sand hill. Nikko ran to catch it, laughing as he rolled it over to Susannah and the others. Mudurra slashed it open with his stone knife. They ate the sweet flesh and Billy and Nikko tried to see how far they could spit the seeds.

Juhi made bracelets of pink shells too. They slid up and down her wrists and ankles as she walked. Faris sat with Nikko, and together they made a whole row of sandcastles, a city of sand that would vanish overnight.

'Jadda?' he asked that night.

'Mmmm?' Jadda sat curled on the cushions, reading her Jane Austen book set in Australia. The house koala sat beside her, chewing on a carrot.

'May I take one of your coconut cakes down to the beach tomorrow? My friends like your cake,' he added.

Jadda looked up from her book. 'Of course. It's good to have friends,' she said quietly. 'Good to do things together. It is good to learn how to be a friend too.' She put her book down. 'I'll make the cake now, so it will be ready for you to take in the morning.'

'Thank you.'

He watched her walk into the kitchen, in the rich red dress that she loved, the gold clips in her dark hair. This was not the grey Jadda, the frightened Jadda of the ship. 'How can I leave you?' whispered Faris. 'How can I bear to leave all this?'

He hadn't gone to listen to David again. The music's beauty was too hard to bear, knowing that it was lost, even if he could still hear it here in this dreamy place. Nor had he asked Jamila, Billy or even Susannah whether he could visit their worlds for a time. Instinctively he knew that the things most treasured would be the things that were most likely to be lost, even if they were to survive the trips back to their own realities.

It was hard enough to bear his own losses; it would be unbearable to wonder which of his new friends' loved memories were lost forever too. Dreams could crack too easily.

Billy was right.

And yet the next afternoon, at last, he climbed the sand hill to sit next to Susannah after lunch, instead of playing the game with the others. She smiled at him without speaking, almost as if she had known that he would sit with her that day. It was a smile of comfort as well as friendship.

For a while they simply looked at the figures playing the game below, set against the white-laced waves. At last she said, 'I liked your cake.'

'Jadda made it. My grandmother.'

'I'd like to meet her again.'

'One day,' he said evasively.

Susannah nodded. 'You're going to leave. You are going to go through the door.'

'I'm not!'

'Not yet. But you will soon.'

'How do you know?' he asked hotly.

'Because you are sitting here with me. The game isn't enough for you any more, nor your memories neither.'

'I can't go back.'

'You can,' she said softly.

'Is this what you did to all the others?' he cried. 'Taunted them?! Persuaded them till they walked through that door?'

'It is.'

'Can't you just leave all of us alone?'

'Should I?' she asked.

He could feel her watching him as he walked down the sand hill to go home.

Days passed. He didn't want to go back! He didn't want to talk about going back with Susannah either. But for some reason he joined her on the sand hill nearly every afternoon now, sitting without speaking, most days, as one by one the others trudged past them when the game was over. None of them met Susannah's eyes as she said her quiet 'good nights'.

She sits here to make us remember, Faris thought.

'Did you do this every day before I came?' he asked suddenly. 'Sit here like a ... a vulture ... to remind them of what they have left?'

'Not every day.' If she felt the insult, she didn't show it. 'Sometimes it's good to live the happiness. Other times are for remembering the hard things and the good. There are seasons for everything.'

'Seasons don't change here.'

'We are the seasons. We come. We go.'

'You know all our stories, don't you?'

She nodded. 'I remember them, so you can all forget. For a while.'

'Doesn't it hurt?'

'Of course it hurts!' she cried. 'Do you think I stay here for the pleasure of it? Don't you think I want a life — my real life, or a chance of one, after all these years?'

'But you stay.'

She nodded, the anger under control again.

'Do you know the story of everyone who has been here?'

Susannah nodded. 'Every one. Jane, Vlad, Mei Ling. I miss Mei Ling,' she added softly.

'Where was she from?'

'There was a war,' said Susannah. 'In a place called Vietnam. Have you heard of it in your time?'

Faris nodded. 'It was a long time ago.'

'Mei Ling and her family escaped, but pirates captured their ship. Took their food, even their water, ripped the jewellery from her mother's ears. Her mother had painted her gold bangles pink with nail polish, so they didn't look like gold, but the pirates took them anyway, even if later they might just throw them in the sea. The pirates took the engine and the fuel. Their boat just floated in the sea. They had no fresh water. Mei Ling's tongue swelled up. She said the sun sucked their life away, till they lay on the deck like dried fish.'

'She went back to that?' Faris wondered at the courage that could take you through a door to a hell of salt and thirst.

Susannah nodded.

'But she was going to die!'

'Mei Ling learned to hope here. She said she had lost the power to hope during the war. She went through the door hoping that it might rain, that a ship might rescue them, or the tide take them to an island.'

A chance — just a chance — of life, thought Faris.

'You must have faith,' said Susannah softly.

'What about Vlad?'

'His country was called Bosnia. Have you heard about it too?'

'A little.' Two religions — or was it two races — who tried to wipe each other out. But that was all he knew.

'Vlad said it was bad when he was small. His father took weapons when they ploughed the fields. His mother was too scared to collect mushrooms in the forest. At last soldiers came from a land called the United Nations. Big men named Maoris. Vlad said the soldiers made so much peace the enemy villages helped each other bring in the harvest. They sang and played music and laughed together after the harvest was brought in. And then the soldiers left.'

'What then?'

'His father woke him in the night. There were screams outside. Scream after scream. Vlad's family hid in the cellar under the apples: his parents, his sister, his grandmother too. The enemy came and kicked the apples above them. They joked that the cowards had fled.

'His family waited three days, hiding under the apples. The fourth night they left, to try to get to a refugee camp in Austria, and then perhaps be selected to come to Australia, where his great-uncle had come after a big war. His family climbed the mountains, using ropes to get down cliffs. Halfway down a cliff his grandmother went limp, like a sausage. They lowered her to the ground. They tried to wake her, but she didn't move even though her eyes were open. Vlad cried, his sister cried, but their grandmother was dead.'

'Vlad told you all of this?'

Susannah nodded. 'He made himself forget. I was afraid he would stay here forever, like Billy, like David and Mudurra. I remembered for him. I remembered how cold he was, like he breathed in ice. The snow began to fall and there was only white. The next step might be safety or a cliff. He couldn't feel his fingers, or his feet. He felt his face vanish ...'

'And then he was here and safe?'

'But he went back.' Susannah's voice was fierce now. 'There was a life waiting for him. I have to hold to that. They made it to a camp in Austria. They have to have had! By now they'll all be together in the real Australia.'

Faris tried to make himself believe it too. 'Where does Jamila come from?' He still knew almost nothing about the tall girl in her scarf.

'Ask her yourself.' Susannah nodded to where Jamila walked up towards the sand hill. She was singing the melody David had played again, but once more the words vanished in the sound of waves and wind.

'I don't want to ... to upset her,' he said reluctantly. In a strange way he almost felt he knew Jamila from David's music. But he had never spoken to her except for words like 'catch' and 'thank you'.

Susannah clenched her hands into small fists. 'But don't you see?! We need to remember, so we can have the courage to survive. We need to remember the people who loved us, the future we might have. Jamila!'

The girl glanced across at them. She stopped singing. For a moment Faris thought she was going to keep walking. Instead she sat next to them.

'You want me to tell Faris my story.'

'How did you know?' he asked.

Jamila smiled, but there was pain in the smile. 'Because that is what Susannah does. She makes me tell my story to everyone. But it hurts to remember.'

The image of a dark wave filled Faris's mind. He blinked. The sand was golden, the sea bright blue again. 'Yes,' he said.

Jamila looked down at the players on the beach, as though looking at them would make the memories less real. 'It would take a hundred years to tell my story properly.' She looked back at Faris. 'I am from a country that you would call Afghanistan. My people are Hazara. The Pashtuns hate Hazara. It has been that way for hundreds of years.' She shrugged slightly. 'I don't even know enough of my story to tell it properly. What makes hate bloom instead of friendship? We are different, but people who are different can be friends. What makes someone say: "Your difference is evil. We will wipe you out, forever"?

'Maybe if I had gone to school I would know the answer. But there was no school for me. My mother went to school. My grandmother was a teacher ...'

'So was mine! But she lost her job.'

'My grandmother lost her school,' said Jamila. 'It was a school for girls. So many girls wanted to go to school that the teachers started classes at dawn, and then the same classes again at lunchtime for another group of students. The teachers worked from first light until the dark. But it was worth it, my grandmother said, because they were bringing light into the lives of their students. Then the Taliban took our town. The Taliban said, "No schools for girls. A girl must stay in her home. The only men she sees must be her family; her only education should be in the proper way to show respect."

'My grandmother covered her whole body, as the Taliban told her to do, in case a man might see her in the courtyard. She stayed inside her house and courtyard. But she sent messages to her students, to come if they wanted to keep learning, to be people, not black-garbed ghosts inside a man's life.

'She taught in her front room. They had no books, only my grandmother's memory. They had no pen and paper — to buy those would make the Taliban suspect.

'But they found out. They cut off her lips.' Jamila was strangely calm. 'Her lips had taught girls improper ways. They cut off her ears, for they had heard improper things. They took out her eyes. They threw her back into her house for my mother to find.

'My grandmother died that night. Her school died with her. My father was angry. He said my grandmother had endangered us all. What did it matter if a girl could not go to school?

'My parents hoped that life would get better. Soldiers came from beyond Afghanistan. I could go outside our house then, but when I heard a shot I had to lie down. You wait for the battle to finish around you, then you get up again.

'Outsiders started a school for girls in our town. I wanted to go, but my father said, "No. Too many people will be angry. She should not go."' Her face twisted. 'He was right. The Taliban poisoned the school's water. Every girl there died. If I had gone there, I would be dead.'

She shrugged. 'That was when my father said that we must leave. My father had heard about Australia, that there is no war, even that people can speak their minds. He did not believe that, but he did believe that in Australia we might be safe. My father does not understand what it is to be a woman, but he cares for his family. Yet there was no way to apply to go to Australia in Afghanistan.

'My father sold our house. We hid among bags of wheat on a truck to Pakistan. We flew to Indonesia. We got on a boat ...'

Faris stared at her in horror. 'Then there was a storm. A wave ...'

She looked at him oddly. 'There was no storm. There was a man. On the first day he was like all the other men, quiet, waiting for the journey to be over. Then he saw my mother look at him, saw her say something to my father.

'The man was Taliban. I don't know why he was on the boat, pretending to be escaping, as we were. But he saw my mother's face. He knew she knew. I saw him give money to the crew. The three crewmen looked at us and nodded. Then the man sat back and smiled. Just a little smile. He was waiting for the night. He would kill us in the darkness, to silence us, as my grandmother had been silenced.

'I prayed that an Australian ship would find us before night came. I prayed that the others on the boat would help us. That night the three of us sat close together. I saw a knife gleam. Then the crew put out the light.'

Her voice still held the same eerie calm. 'I heard the man come towards us, the rustle of his clothing. I thought, please let our boat land on Australia now!

'And then I woke up,' said Jamila. 'I woke up and there were my clothes, ready for school.'

She looked at Faris. 'It was a long time before I remembered. Life is good here. My mother is happy. Late every afternoon I go to school, with the second lot of students. I study. But I never learn more than I knew before. When I realised that, I cried. I cannot even tell my mother the school is not really there. I never had much to lose before,' she added. 'Just my family and my life. A little life. Then I dreamed what life might be, a free life in Australia. I have that life here. So now I don't remember. If I can.'

Faris stared at her in wonder. He had felt that his grey boat was the only one going to Australia. Oh, he had known there had been others, that their rusty craft had even made other voyages before theirs. But for the first time he felt the thousands of years, the countless shadowy faces of those who had sought refuge, who had dreamed of a place over the sea's horizon that they called Australia or Botany Bay or even, like Mudurra, just the land beyond the smoke on the horizon.

'So will you stay here forever?'

Jamila gave Susannah a wry smile. 'No. One day I will be my grandmother's child. One day I'll have the courage to go back through the door.'

She stood up. 'But not today. Not for a long, long time, I think. Maybe my family will survive. Or maybe this is the only Australia I will ever see. This afternoon I will go to school again. I will learn nothing, but I will feel that I have. Tonight my mother and I will read together, with no fear of shots in the darkness or strangers at the door.' She smiled at them, then strode off down the sand hill, the ends of her scarf flying in the wind.

Faris lay that night in his clean sheets in his bright bedroom. Am I a coward? Is Jamila a coward too?

No, he thought. We aren't cowards as long as we do go back one day. Back to the Taliban man with the knife, back to the wave. Back to those we love.

'One day I'll have the courage,' Jamila had said. Would he find the courage one day too?

'How many have come here?' he asked Susannah the next afternoon. He had climbed up the sand hill to join her. It was almost a ritual now. He still wasn't sure why he did it — sit with a girl, and a young one at that.

But Susannah *wasn't* a little girl. He had the feeling that even when she had been, when she had first come here, Susannah had been different.

Of all of them, Susannah had a more certain future to go back to. Yet she had chosen to stay here, to guard and help the others and to guide them back. What had given a girl strength to do that?

Susannah took her book out of the pocket of her apron and handed it to him. 'Twenty-six. Count the names, if you like.'

Faris opened the book. He stared at the careful, rounded printing. 'All of the others went back through the door?'

'They have. Some went back the first day. As though they just needed a few minutes to catch their breath, to get their thoughts clear, then dive back to where they'd been. Billy is so sore when that happens.' She looked indulgently down at her friend, jumping high to grab the ball from the air. 'Arrivals are really the only changes in our lives.'

'How often do new people come?'

'Now that I can't be telling you. I try to keep track of days. But someone will come, and say it's 1930, and two days later another will be from 1945. I don't know if time is different here, or if it's me and I can't keep it straight.'

She looked at Faris squarely. 'Not that it matters. You go back to when you came from, no matter what happens here.'

'Juhi thinks she can go back with Mudurra.'

Susannah shrugged. 'Who knows?' She grinned at him. 'I have the question you should be asking. Why is there such a terrible lot of hating in the world? Why do we hate so much that we try to kill those who aren't like us?'

'I don't know.'

'Sometimes I'm thinking that we need to love more. That if enough of us do good things, it might balance out the hate. Nikko!' Susannah's voice changed as the small boy climbed the sand hill. 'Are you going home early?'

The little boy nodded. 'There is stifado tonight. The best stifado in Australia.'

'Tell Faris what stifado is like.'

Nikko considered. 'Good,' he replied, as though that was all that was needed to be said.

Susannah laughed. 'Tell Faris about your mam then.'

'She is just a woman,' said Nikko. He paused and added, 'But she makes the best stifado in our village. Everybody says so.'

'Every night?'

Nikko nodded. 'I have to go,' he said quickly. 'She'll have dinner ready.' He ran over the sand hill.

Faris looked at Susannah. 'You'd make a little boy leave all this, to drown in the sea?'

'You think it's better to be six years old forever?' she asked hotly. 'To live the same days over and over?'

'But what if you're wrong? What if we just go back to our deaths? Or even if some of us survive and others die? How can you be so sure?'

He looked at Susannah again. 'You're not sure,' he said.

'No.' She met his gaze. 'Some nights I'm crying myself to sleep, knowing what I've sent a child back to. But we can only do what we think is right, Faris. So this is what I do. It is the hardest thing in the world sometimes. But I think that what I do is right.' She gazed at the doorway, the driftwood of its arch becoming darker as the shadows grew. 'I had a friend once,' she said softly.

'Aren't we all your friends?'

She smiled at that, rubbing the tears from her cheeks. 'There are many kinds of friends. Bridget was like me. Ten years old, from Ireland. She was here when I arrived. She knew what I was feeling. It's how we all feel when we first get here. Happy at first, thinking that somehow we've broken free and made it to Australia. And then day after day unfolds, and suddenly we realise that what we have left is still waiting for us, that the place we have come to will never change.

'Bridget was here for me, when I remembered. I sat here on the sand, right where we sit now. Trembling and shaking and crying I was, and she held me and stroked my hair.'

'Was she from your time too?'

Susannah shook her head. 'From long before me. 1849 she said she sailed in a ship of rotting wood from Galway. It was the potato famine. Have you ever heard of that?'

Faris shook his head.

'The English owned the land. We Irish rented what was once our own. In Bridget's time there were only potatoes to eat and milk from a cow. But then a disease killed all the potatoes, made them rot in the ground. All you could smell was the rot, she said. And then you could smell the death too, as people starved. Whole villages, too weak to leave their doorsteps. Bodies in the lanes and gutters.

'Her mam had a gold ring. They sold it for passage to Australia. America was cheaper and not so far, but her mam's brother had gone to Australia and she thought he might give them a home. Anyhow the ships to America were all full and they had no more money to feed the family till a passage could be found, only a sackful of potatoes that had escaped the blight. And that sack had to feed the family as they travelled to Australia.

'They lived on those potatoes, she said, half cooked because that made the hunger less. They were halfway across the ocean when there were no more potatoes. The captain wouldn't give them food. He said they had paid for their passage and no more; there was no food for the likes of them. They lay there in the dark belly of the ship and felt the hunger take them. She woke up here.'

'What sort of Australia had she imagined?'

'Like mine, it was. All her family safe. Puddings on the table, potatoes mashed with butter, big white loaves of bread, a bucket of milk with cream rising to the top.'

'But she left.'

'She did that. Stayed with me till I'd stopped my crying. Days or weeks or months, who knows how long? That last day I walked to the doorway with her. I watched her pull that skin back and just for a glimpse I saw it, smelled the stench of dying, saw the white faces in the dark.'

'She went back to that?' asked Faris slowly.

'She did. But she wasn't the girl who came here. "I'm not going to lie there in the darkness," she said to me. "I'll not let that captain win. We'll take his plum puddings and his salt beef, and if we can't, I'll catch rats and make the cook boil them on the stove. But I'll get us to Australia even if we have to eat the rats. You'll see."'

'Do you think she did?'

'I saw her face that day. I knew that death itself would give way to her, at least for a while, till she'd got

124

her family to Australia. They'd given up, you see, from all the losses, with the hunger and the smell of death. But Bridget found her courage again here.'

'Did you have other friends?'

'Mei Ling. Jane was a friend too for a while — she was English, but from a place called Singapore,' Susannah said quietly. 'Japanese soldiers invaded. They bombed the ship when she and her mam tried to escape. Their planes shot at them in the water, as they tried to swim to shore. Jane swam through blood. Then she was here.'

'But she went back?'

'I stood with her as she went through the door too. I'd told her about Bridget, how staying here had made her strong. Jane said that she wouldn't die neither. She wouldn't give in, till she and her mam were safe. And I have to think she did.'

She stood up. It seemed to Faris that she stood as the old woman she should be, not as a ten-year-old girl. 'No, I'm not just thinking it. I know it. I've seen their faces as they go. Ah Goon and Jane, Bridget and Mei Ling, Big Johnny and Abdulla ... I saw their faces, every one. They were the faces of those who will survive,' said Susannah fiercely. 'That's what this place has given them. A refuge, a space to learn what they need to know about themselves.'

'But some won't go. Some *shouldn't* go.' Faris nodded at the players on the beach.

'They'll go some day,' said Susannah. Suddenly her voice was weary. 'Every one of them. Then at last I can go as well. You'll be goin' next. Good night, Faris,' she added. 'May good angels watch over your dreams.'

Faris watched her walk down the sand hill, watched the lamp come on in the stone cottage, heard the long low sound he supposed came from a cow. He looked away, back to the beach for a second. When he looked down the hill again, it was his own street before him.

He walked down the sand hill and put on his shoes. She was right. Impossible, arrogant, impudent small girl, but she was right.

One day soon he would go back. He'd face the wave with Jadda once again.

One day. Not yet.

CHAPTER 12

'Want to see my farm, matey?' asked Billy casually next afternoon.

Faris hesitated, curiosity warring with wariness, remembering Billy's talk of cut-throats and knives. Billy's world might be frightening. 'All right,' he said at last.

Billy laughed. 'Don't worry, matey. Ain't no tigers there to bite you. Ain't no coves with knives to stab you in the guts neither. All's sweet as apple pie.'

They walked up the beach, leaving the others to the game. Susannah nodded as they passed.

'Want to come too?' asked Billy.

She smiled. 'Not today.'

Faris looked down. Billy's world was already there: a narrow dirt road with neat hedges on either side of it. Fat cows and sheep so white they looked like clouds grazed on one side of the road. On the other side a big three-storey stone house with at least a dozen chimneys sat among fruit trees — apples, pears, peaches and others Faris didn't know all laden with fruit.

'Are your parents there?'

Billy grinned. It wasn't a happy grin. For the first time Faris saw that several of his back teeth were missing as well as the one in front. 'Ain't got no parents.

I were a workhouse brat, till I was sold to Mr Hallop. He were the best dabs in the street. Pickpocket,' he added when he saw that Faris didn't understand. 'He taught the whole gang of us brats to pick pockets too. Give geezers a cosh in a dark alley too.'

'A cosh?'

'Bashed 'em on the head,' said Billy cheerfully. 'I was good at it. Thought I'd 'ave me own gang one day. But Spriggy Pierce were jealous of me. Turned me in to the Bow Street Runners when I had this cove's watch on me. I were lucky to only get seven years, and not the gallows.'

Faris stared at him, then at the farm below. Billy was a thief! Not just a thief, but a violent one. He might even be a murderer.

Did he want to go into the world of a thief?

'Race you to the front door!' yelled the bigger boy. He ran down the slope, leaping over the hedge instead of going through the gate.

Faris glanced back at Susannah. 'It's safe,' she said. Once again she almost seemed to know what he was thinking. 'Billy's changed, since he's been here. He won't hurt you.'

Faris hesitated. He'd look like a coward if he didn't follow. Billy might be angry too. He ran down the sand hill and up the road. The boy waited at the front door for Faris to catch up to him.

'Aren't you going to open the door?' Faris looked at the big iron-bolted front door warily.

'Nah. Why should I? Got servants for that.' As he spoke, the door opened. A young girl in a bright white apron dropped a curtsey. 'Welcome home, young master,' she said to Billy.

'Master!' said Faris.

Billy grinned. 'That's it, matey. That I am.'

'She has to do everything you tell her to?'

Billy looked at him, suddenly fierce. 'Don't you be thinking I don't treat me servants well. They eat as good as me. A cut off the roast for dinner and a bed to themselves, aye, and a bedroom to themselves too, with a fire in it, an' sheets and everything. It's a good life for all of us.'

He led the way into the house and down a wide passageway with paintings of cows and horses in big gold frames on either side. Two young men in striped silk trousers and white wigs bowed as he and Faris passed. 'Welcome, master,' said one of them.

Billy ignored them. 'Come down to the kitchen. We could eat in one o' the dining rooms — I got two o' them, great big dining tables, silver candlesticks an' all — an' me butler could serve us — but the kitchen's better.'

Faris nodded uncomfortably. A world where Billy was master, where everyone did as Billy said. Billy, the thief. Billy, perhaps a murderer.

He didn't like it.

The kitchen was stone-walled, with full shelves and a big wooden table. A fat woman in a striped apron and cap looked up from kneading dough as they came through the door. Behind her a big hunk of meat roasted on a spit over the fire, next to a big black oven. The woman smiled. 'Welcome home, master. Welcome to your friend too.'

'This here is Far Eyes.' Billy grinned at her. 'Far Eyes, this is Mrs Bonnet, me cook. Mrs Bonnet makes the best ginger nuts in the whole world.'

Faris wondered what a ginger nut was. 'Pleased to meet you,' he said politely.

'Now you sit down.' Mrs Bonnet pulled out a chair for him. 'I've got a nice apple pie ready in the oven, and a good hunk of cheese to eat with it. Put your feet up by the fire. Mabel!' she yelled to someone in the next room. 'Bring the apple juice for the master and his friend.'

Mrs Bonnet eyed Billy's red trousers. 'They're damp,' she said sharply. 'You been paddling in the water?'

'No, Mrs Bonnet.' Billy tried to look concerned.

Mrs Bonnet snorted. 'And the mice are going to dance at suppertime. You go and change them wet trousers now, you hear? I don't want you catching cold.'

'But Mrs Bonnet —'

'Now don't you argue. The pie will be out of the oven when you get back. And there's mutton chops, just the way you like them, and baked potatoes and jam buns. Off you go. Shoo!'

'Won't be long.' Billy looked half embarrassed, half the most content that Faris had ever seen him.

Faris looked back at Mrs Bonnet, lifting her pie from the big black oven as Billy went upstairs. What had his friend's life been, growing up on the streets, grabbing what he could?

'Have to look after the lad,' said Mrs Bonnet. 'Make sure he eats right, feed him up. Needs looking after, he does.'

Faris smiled. This was the heart of Billy's world.

The pickpocket might not know it, but Faris had just met Billy's mum.

CHAPTER 13

He went to Jamila's world the next day.

'No,' said Jamila, as he ran after her as she walked up the beach to the sand hill and asked if he could come with her.

'Why not?'

Jamila didn't look at him. 'Because I say so.'

Suddenly Faris felt he understood. 'Your father wouldn't like you bringing a strange boy home, would he? Nor your brothers. Even if we just walked through the street together, someone might tell them.'

For the first time Jamila looked him straight in the face. 'You think my father might whip me? Men might whisper, "Look at that girl, she walks with a boy along the street"?'

'Maybe,' said Faris cautiously.

Jamila began to stride up the sand hill. 'Then you can come with me.'

Faris hurried after her. Jamila nodded to Susannah as they passed.

Susannah stared at Faris. 'You're not taking him, are you?'

Jamila laughed. It was a good laugh, like the wind. 'Why not?'

'Because ...' Susannah stopped.

Faris looked from one girl to another. 'What's wrong with Jamila's world? Have you been there?'

'Not a thing wrong with it,' said Susannah cheerfully. 'And I've been there, though Billy hasn't, nor David. You have a nice time of it.' She grinned.

Faris took another three steps behind Jamila, then looked down.

The city was white. The tiny houses in Nikko's world had been white. But this city was built of marble, almost as glowing as the sun.

Flowers lined the road, small flowers like a carpet, trees with garlands of flowers hanging from their branches. Every house was two storeys tall, flat-roofed, with low-walled courtyards. Fountains bubbled gently, set among a mosaic of coloured tiles. Apricot trees with small speckled fruit sheltered white stone benches, where girls in silk headscarves and bright dresses bent over books, or wrote at marble tables.

He looked around at the hills. Tall white spires almost reached the sky. A school, he thought. Or a university.

'Are you coming?' called Jamila.

Faris looked at the courtyards. Each one was different. This one had a large fountain, this one a big domed outside oven. Even the patterns of the tiles were different.

He shook his head. His own world was so limited compared to hers, the same house over and over again. He looked down at the flowers at his feet. Each one had eight petals. Each was perfect, its perfume wafting up.

'Faris!' called Jamila.

He hurried after her.

They walked along the street together. The houses gave way to a marketplace. Women in bright embroidered headscarves offered pastries to other women, and small cups of tea that smelled of mint or cardamom, or hot sweet milk. Spices spilled out of sacks. Faris recognised cinnamon, nutmeg, saffron, but there were tens of others he didn't know. Two strong women hauled wooden paddles topped with just-cooked flat bread out of a rounded earth oven. Another woman stirred chunks of chicken in a giant wok.

'Where are we going? Your house?'

'No,' said Jamila.

A woman in a dress of bright blue edged with gold embroidery and a coin necklace offered them a tray of silver-and-enamel bowls of apricots and pistachios, a silver plate covered with a paste of what looked like nuts and raisins, and another silver plate piled with tiny pastries. *'KhoDa PushTho PaNai Tho,'* she said.

Jamila stopped and took a pastry. 'Thank you. Try one,' she said to Faris. 'It's good.'

Faris bit into the pastry as they walked. It *was* good — almonds, honey and spices, sweet and savoury at the same time. All around them women offered bolts of silk, carpets, scarves …

Women, he thought. This is a city of women.

He glanced at Jamila. She grinned. 'There are no men to be afraid of here. No father or uncles to obey.'

'No men at all?'

Jamila shook her head.

'You've never asked Billy here? Or David?'

'No.'

'Don't you think you can trust them?'

'Of course I can trust them! David is one of the best people I have ever met. He took my poem and made it music!' Jamila stopped and looked at the ground, as though realising what she had just said. 'Yes,' she whispered. 'I can trust them. I trust you too.' She nodded, to herself as much as to him. 'One day I'll ask them here.'

They walked on together. Up on a green hill above the houses girls flew kites, as bright as their scarves. At last they paused before the building with tall spires. Jamila led the way up white marble stairs.

Faris expected a big hall, like the theatre where David played. But instead they were in a small foyer, with an ordinary door at the other end.

Jamila opened it. Faris followed her inside.

It was a classroom, but not like any he had seen.

The room was long. Rich rugs hung from white walls, in between shelf after shelf of books. The floor was covered in rugs, but also cushions, silky and rounded and comfortable looking, and on the cushions were girls, happy girls in bright dresses and brighter headscarves, each with books or slates in their hands.

At the far end of the room was a blackboard, and by the blackboard was a teacher, a tall woman with a headscarf just like Jamila's, and lines of laughter around her eyes. She smiled as Faris and Jamila slid into seats at the back.

'Today,' said the teacher, 'we will learn about the most important number of all. It is zero. Can anyone tell me why we call it "zero"?'

Jamila put up her hand. 'The great Arabian mathematician Mohammed ibn-Musa al-Khwarizmi called it "sifr". All other nations took the name. He was the first to use zero in equations. "Algorithms" are called after him, but people mispronounce his name just as they mispronounced "sifr".'

'Correct.' The teacher looked at her approvingly. 'It is so easy to make a mistake when you are remembering lessons from long ago. It is as easy to say that "sifr" is "zero" as it is to say girls should not study mathematics.'

The girls all laughed, as though saying 'girls shouldn't study mathematics' was the funniest joke they'd ever heard.

The teacher grinned. 'Now who can tell me three different ways to use a zero?'

Faris knew the answer. He'd known about Mohammed ibn-Musa al-Khwarizmi too. But he waited as Jamila put up her hand, as her grandmother — for surely this teacher was the grandmother Jamila had known when she was a little girl — nodded at Jamila to tell the class. This was Jamila's world, her city of women.

Jadda would like this teacher, he thought. He wished that they could meet. Maybe if he thought hard enough, if Jamila did too …

No. Even if the two women came together in his imagination, they couldn't really meet. Jamila's grandmother was dead; his own was lost in what had become a never-ending moment as he waited for the wave to crash down.

For a second he almost felt the coldness of the sea again. Then he was back, in the white-walled classroom, in Jamila's city of women.

Darkness rested like a cashmere blanket on the marble-walled city as he and Jamila walked back towards the beach. They stopped by the sand hill. 'I'll go home from here,' said Jamila. 'My mother will be waiting.'

Faris hesitated. 'Jamila ... you said David gave you music for your poem. Is that the song you sing, down on the beach?'

'Yes.'

'I've heard him play it. It sounds ... it feels almost like my story. Hatred and loss ...'

'It isn't your song. It's mine. I wrote it for my grandmother. It is a song for women. Not men.'

'But David plays it. Please — would you sing it for me now?'

He could see when trust edged out the last hesitation from her heart.

Her voice was small and sweet.

'I am a woman, I'm easy to kill,
A gun in the face or a rape for the thrill.
I am a woman, and I'll never die,
Steal my lips and you'll still hear my cry.
Words that are whispered, from mother to child,
I am a woman. We all are mankind.'

The wind from the sea seemed to sing the last words again. Faris felt tears prickle. 'Jamila?'

'Yes?'

'Your song. It is a song for men too. For everyone who is hated. We all are mankind.'

She looked at him without speaking. 'Maybe that is why David could give it music,' she said at last. 'Good night, Faris. And thank you.'

'What for?'

'For showing me that a man can walk in the city of women. You, David, Billy, perhaps even my father, and other men too. I wrote the words, but I didn't understand them. We share more than divides us.'

She vanished into the dark. Faris waited a minute, in case she came back, then walked up the sand hill and turned to go home.

CHAPTER 14

He drank in each detail every day now. Every hug from Jadda, the bright Jadda with laughing eyes he had recreated from so long before. The softness of his bed at night, the safe bed where no men with clubs and pistols would drag you from your sleep.

He breathed in the beauty of the beach. He looked at his friends too. Because they *were* friends: little Nikko, strong Jamila, Billy, who he had thought a bully, but who was trying his best to defend them all. Susannah, who held their memories for them until they were needed, who held their pain till one day they could bear it again. Over near the far cliff Mudurra sat with Juhi, carving out fish hooks from the flat pink shells.

On the day Faris stepped through that driftwood door he would lose them all. Never see Susannah's small, fierce face. Probably never see a fish hook carved from shell either. They would be separated by time, as well as space. If they survived at all.

If only I could step back through the doorway if I needed to, he thought. If only whenever you thought, I can't do this, you could just step back through and play on the beach, till you had gathered your strength again.

Yet in his heart he knew that this was a gift that could be given only once. Perhaps, when you had stepped through, you had no need for the doorway, for by then you would have truly chosen real life.

Even the game was precious now. Somehow every time you threw a ball to someone and every time they caught it or threw it to you, a small thread was made between the players.

The game had been fun this morning. It was always fun. Jamila had brought down lamb on skewers at midday, with chunks of fat in between the meat that spat and hissed as it cooked over Mudurra's fire, and flat bread, still warm from the oven. There were jugs of pomegranate juice, chilled with snow, bowls of apricots, big floury ones and tiny ones that spurted juice when you bit into them, and tiny yellow grapes and a bowl of pistachio nuts. The grape seeds floated when a laughing Nikko spat them into the sea.

Susannah and Jamila gathered up the bowls as the others began to play again. Faris held the ball, hot from the sand, in his hands, and wondered who to throw it to. David, he thought.

But David stared at the waves.

'David!' Faris called impatiently.

David shook his head. 'Look!'

Something thrashed in the water between the beach and the rocks. For a moment Faris wondered if it was a shark, or a giant fish. Then a dark head gasped for air. It vanished below the waves.

Faris glanced at the others. But we are all here, he

thought, safe on the beach. Susannah was desperately counting them all.

'Who's out there?' he demanded breathlessly.

'I don't know!' Susannah's voice didn't quite hide her fear. 'No one ever arrives from the sea! They come over the sand hill, like you did.'

The waves splashed about Faris's ankles. Without realising it, they had all run down into the water. He stopped as the waves broke about his knees. He saw the others stop too.

Mudurra was the only one of them who could swim — even Juhi only splashed in the shallows. The young man strode further out, into the sea. He dived down into the waves. Only his dark head and arms were visible, swimming out towards the place where the figure had vanished.

'Help him!' Juhi looked pleadingly at the others. 'He's going to his death out there.'

'How can we help?' asked Faris, as Billy said, 'He can swim, can't he?' Faris had never heard Billy's voice sound uncertain before.

'Not against the current out there! Not near the rocks!'

'She's right. Mudurra says the current is deadly. He tried to swim against it before you came. He nearly died. He says the next time it will kill him.' Suddenly Faris felt it was hard to breathe. It was as though he too was underwater, like the stranger out at sea, as though the wave had crashed over him already.

He couldn't let the stranger suffer like that. He couldn't let Mudurra be swept out to whatever strange ocean lay beyond their guarding rocks. But how could they help him, and help whoever was struggling in the water, if they couldn't swim?

'A boat,' said Billy, his voice still wobbly. 'We need to fetch a boat.'

'Where from?' demanded Faris. 'Do you have a boat?'

Billy shook his head. Of course not, thought Faris, staring out at the strange figure still struggling in the water, at Mudurra's dark head moving towards what he must know would only be a temporary rescue, till both he and the stranger in the water were swept out to sea. There are no boats in the worlds we have created. Boats mean fear for us, not safety.

'A bridge.' Faris heard his own voice speak almost before he thought the words. He looked at the others impatiently. 'We can put a plank or a ladder across from the cliff to the first rock, and then from the first rock to the second. Then as they are swept out to the rocks, we reach down and grab them.'

It was so easy to say. But would it work? It has to work, he thought.

'I can get a ladder from home —' began Billy.

'No!' Would a ladder from an imaginary world work on the beach? Nor was there time to fetch one.

Faris gazed frantically along the sand. But there was nothing that could make a bridge, just the small bits of driftwood, fit only for a fire, the seaweed, the basket and juice jugs from their lunch ...

Out among the waves Mudurra had reached the spot where the swimmer had vanished. His head ducked below the water. Juhi began to wade further out towards him. Susannah held her back. 'No! You aren't strong enough!'

'I have to!'

'Then Mudurra would have to rescue you too!' said Billy.

Jamila turned to Susannah. 'We have to use the wood from the doorway.'

'No!' Susannah's face was white under her freckles.

'They're the only long pieces of wood on the beach.'

'We can put the doorway back together again.' Faris didn't know if they could. But it was their only hope of rescuing the two struggling swimmers.

Out in the froth of water Mudurra's face popped up again. He gasped, then sank.

Suddenly Susannah gave a small savage nod. She began to run. The others ran with her. David reached the doorway first. He pulled at one half of the giant driftwood arch, heedless of splinters in his long white musician's fingers.

The doorframe didn't move.

Faris grabbed it too. Hands covered his — white, brown, olive, freckled ...

'On the count of three!' yelled Billy. 'One, two, *three*.'

They pushed. The wood shifted slightly.

Faris shot a desperate glance out to the bay. 'He's surfaced!' as Mudurra's face emerged again. This time he held what looked to be a shapeless bundle of grey clothes.

'Push!' screamed Juhi, her small hands making no difference to the wood of the doorway.

'All together!' Billy took command. 'One. Two. Three!'

And suddenly the doorway fell, so easily, so simply, that it seemed impossible that this had ever been anything more than two hunks of driftwood with a skin flapping between.

But there was no time to think about that now. Faris and Billy heaved the first hunk of driftwood between them, while Jamila and David lifted the other, leaving the skin where it had fallen. For a few seconds Nikko tried to help, but it was obvious that he was just getting in the way.

Faris was dimly aware of Susannah sitting Nikko on the sand, telling him to wait, to be a good wee boyo; out in the water Mudurra struggled to keep the stranger's face turned up to the air, his strong body already being swept towards the rocks.

'Hurry!' shrieked Juhi.

'I will pray to St Kangarou.' Nikko sounded like he was trying not to cry.

'Pray to God for all of us,' said Susannah, as Juhi ran around to the cliff and scrambled over the rocks, then held out her arms to take the first bit of bridging wood.

Would the length of driftwood be long enough to reach to the first rock? It has to be! thought Faris. No time for any other plan now.

He and Juhi thrust the wood towards the first rock. Billy and David steadied it behind. For a heart-stopping second he was sure it would be too short. Then the end met the rock.

'Now to carry the other one out there,' panted Billy. He glanced doubtfully down at the ancient driftwood. 'Dunno how much weight it'll hold.'

'Then I'll be the one going across it first.' Before they could stop her, Susannah had run onto the driftwood bridge, as though the thin wood was a broad and sturdy staircase.

The wind pushed and pulled at her long dress, almost unbalancing her. She leaped towards the rock, as though in challenge to the elements.

She was across.

'Pass the other over to me!' she yelled. But Juhi and Jamila were already heaving the wood across the gap. Susannah grabbed it, then managed to push it onto the second rock.

'If it will take Susannah, it will take me,' said Jamila. She stepped like a tightrope walker onto the driftwood, her arms out to balance her. Juhi waited till she was across, then followed her.

Faris glanced at Billy and David. They were heavier than the girls, especially Billy. Should they risk the driftwood breaking?

'If one bit o' wood breaks, they can use the other,' said Billy shortly. 'Them girls don't have the strength to pull Mudurra up by themselves.'

If the driftwood broke under them, they might drown. But there was no time to weigh the risk.

One by one the boys edged across to the closest rock, first Faris, then David. The girls had already crossed to the second. Faris held his breath as Billy came last, cautiously, foot by foot. But the driftwood didn't break.

The rock felt cold under Faris's feet. It should be warm from the sun, like the sand, he thought. Somehow he knew the water would be cold too.

It was easier crossing the second bridge. The six of them clustered together, on the second rock. It was as level as it had seemed from the beach, as if it had been carved. They were about two metres higher than the surging water below. The beach and tiny Nikko looked strangely distant, as though they had travelled much further than a few minutes' run.

Faris looked down into the water. Mudurra had seen them. He was trying to swim towards their rock as the current swept him out, dragging the limp figure of the stranger with him.

Closer, closer ... Faris could see both faces now: Mudurra's grim; the other a girl with dark skin, black hair and a bulk of grey wet clothes.

Juhi kneeled down and stretched out her arms. She gave a cry. 'We're too high up! He won't be able to reach us!'

'Maybe Billy can lean right down ...' began Faris.

'I still won't be able to grab him,' said Billy. 'Not from up here. We need a rope.'

'We don't have one!'

Billy gave a short hard grin. 'Who says?' He tore at the buttons of his shirt. 'Here, take your shirt off. An' you too,' he said to David, already tying the sleeves of his shirt to Faris's.

Would the shirts be long enough? Would Mudurra have the strength to grab them, carrying his limp burden too? Could a rope of shirts hold to pull them upwards?

Mudurra no longer struggled against the current, but was letting it take him, using what was left of his strength to keep the girl's face out of the water. A few more minutes and they would be between the rocks.

Find something that floats, said a whisper in his mind. It was Jadda's voice — the grey Jadda, the Jadda on the grey boat.

The water bladders. Faris remembered how Nikko had blown them up, how they had popped.

Even as he thought it, he was running, scrambling across the two driftwood bridges, leaping the rocks, along the beach, back to the fire and the remnants of their meal. Now and then he risked a second's glance. Mudurra was close to the rocks now, the girl still in his arms, the others crowded on the second rock, their yells of encouragement almost lost in the wind.

We have been children playing on a beach, he thought, even as his hands busied themselves emptying the bladders, blowing them up, tying them together with Mudurra's plaited string. But now we are no longer lost children. We are the rescuers ...

Perhaps.

He ran back, pushing his feet into the wet sand, urging his body harder than he ever had before.

Faster! Faster! The bladders bounced behind him. The sun and sea wind burned his body. He had never gone bare-chested outdoors before.

Faris hesitated only briefly at the driftwood bridge, then wobbled his way across it. He had walked up paths as narrow. No reason to step sideways now, slip into the dark deep water, be swept out, swept under, lost in the dark wave.

The first rock was cold again under his feet. He balanced his way over the next bridge. Jamila reached out a hand to guide him, then he was among the others.

He looked down. Was he too late?

Mudurra was almost at the rock, his eyes fixed, determined, his mouth gasping for air, swimming like a frog, kicking out with both legs, balanced on the water. The girl was a froth of grey clothes and black seaweed ...

Was she still breathing?

'Where's Billy?' Faris panted.

Susannah pointed mutely down.

For a moment Faris thought she meant Billy had fallen off the rock. Then he saw that the convict boy had tied one end of the shirt-rope around himself, while Juhi and David held the other end. Billy dangled half in the water as he reached out his arms to the swimmers.

'Here!' Faris yelled. He dangled the bladders down to Billy. 'They'll stop you from sinking!'

Billy's face looked up, grim-faced with terror, but his hands didn't shake as he reached up to take the bladders.

'Pass some to Mudurra too!'

Faris watched as Billy rested his weight on half the floating bladders, then threw the others towards Mudurra. It was an accurate throw. How many years had Billy spent throwing a ball?

Billy is the strongest of us, thought Faris, but someone lighter should have gone down. Billy might be too heavy for us to haul up, with the weight of wet cloth too. What if the current is too strong for us, and rips him and the rope out of our hands?

And suddenly he had the solution to that too. 'Susannah! Jamila! Help me!'

'How?'

'Pull both lots of driftwood over here. Don't worry, we won't lose them.' I hope, he thought, imagining them all stranded on the rock. 'Now tie the last sleeve around them. See? If we push the driftwood over the other end of the rock, their weight should stop Billy from being swept away.'

And if just one of our shirts tears, Billy will die, he thought. Mudurra and the girl will die. Our bridge will be lost. We will all be stranded here till we die.

They rolled the hunks of driftwood across the rock, then pushed them over the other side. For a moment the lengths of wood swung back and forth, then dangled down.

The shirts and driftwood held.

Now, for a while, Billy was secure. Faris squeezed past Susannah and Jamila to the other side of the rock, just as Mudurra's hand met Billy's. For a second it looked like Mudurra would be swept away, through the rocks and out to sea. Then Billy had him gripped by both his wrists, while Mudurra held the girl.

And now to get them up.

'Strip off her clothes, you fools!' yelled Jamila, Jamila the modest, Jamila the strong. She untied her headscarf. Her hair blew wild and free as she dangled the headscarf down. The breeze blew it back at her. Then suddenly the wind dropped, for a moment, and the scarf became a rope too. Billy grabbed it, using it to steady himself in the rage of water.

Mudurra was already tearing at the girl's clothes. The garments drifted for a metre, like sodden seaweed, then sank, as Billy and Mudurra tied the scarf-rope around the girl.

'Pull!' screamed Billy.

They pulled.

The girl came up like a saturated teddy bear, like wet washing. Like a body, thought Faris, then thrust the thought away. She had to be alive. Hands reached for her as she neared the top of the rock.

She was fifteen, perhaps, a couple of years older than him, white underclothes against a dark skin, a long black plait; she was so thin her ankles and wrists were no thicker than Susannah's.

Her eyes were shut. She didn't breathe.

'Stand clear.' Faris bent down and began to breathe into the girl's mouth. His father had taught him this, so many, many years before. He had almost forgotten till now.

What if he did it wrong?

It felt strange feeling a girl's lips against his. They were soft and cold. He breathed out again, trying to remember how his father had taught him to count. Wasn't he supposed to press her heart too?

Suddenly the girl gave a heaving breath. Faris automatically rolled her on her side, just as she vomited seawater over the black rock. She lay there, giving short hard pants, her eyes closed. Alive.

Faris turned back to find Mudurra clambering up behind him, his feet against the rock, using the shirt-rope to haul and guide himself. For a second Mudurra stood there, glistening and black, triumphant above the water, then he dropped exhausted into a surprisingly small heap on the rock.

'Mudurra!' Juhi bent over him. His hand came up and touched her cheek, as he gasped strength back into his body.

'Billy?' Faris peered down. Billy bobbed in the water, buoyed by the water bladders. The current tore at him, the waves slapped him, but he held the shirt-rope fast.

'Haul me up, matey!' he yelled.

'We're trying!' David and the others were already pulling. But even their desperate strength and the anchor of the driftwood wasn't enough to haul up a waterlogged Billy.

'Well, I ain't goin' to let the sea take me. If a darkie can walk up a rock, then so can I.'

Billy reached up one hand and grabbed the shirt-rope higher up. He let go of the floating bladders and gripped with the other hand too, forcing his feet against the rock.

Once again he let go with one hand, reached it higher up to grab the rope, then walked his legs, his sodden-trousered, heavy legs, up the rock ...

And stopped halfway. His whole body seemed to tremble. Strength of will had got Billy this far.

But it was not enough.

'Hold my legs!' Juhi lay down on the rock's edge, her arms reaching for Billy, as David and Faris grabbed her. Now Mudurra panted as he seized her ankles too.

Slowly Billy emerged, like a red-and-white fish, streaming and gasping. 'Took youse long enough,' he said. And fainted.

CHAPTER 15

It was David who grabbed the rope so that the driftwood bridge didn't fall into the sea, Susannah and David who hauled up the driftwood, while Juhi hugged Mudurra, and Faris held the girl's head steady in case she vomited again and choked. Billy gasped beside them, slowly coming round from his faint.

At last Faris and Susannah guided the length of wood back to make a bridge to the other rock. Faris crossed first, then held out his hands to steady David and Jamila as they helped Billy across, holding onto the shirt-rope, stretched tight between Faris on one rock and Susannah on the other to steady them in case one of them fell.

They didn't.

Mudurra came next, swiftly, surely, even though his hands still trembled, then Faris went back to help Susannah and Juhi carry the limp weight of the semi-conscious girl. The girls had dressed her in one of Susannah's petticoats, her shawl and apron. They pushed the second length of driftwood over to the cliff. Slowly, one by one, they made it from the first rock back to the shore.

The bridges held.

Faris was glad that the girl was clothed, not for his own embarrassment — that seemed to have been long blown out to sea — but for her sake, so that when she properly woke she would know she had not been handled naked by strange boys.

The girl muttered something. Her eyes didn't open. But she breathed.

Between them, Faris, Jamila and David managed to carry her to the beach, to lie her on the warm sand, her head cradled in Jamila's lap.

Little Nikko ran to them. He grabbed Susannah's hand, then peered at the strange girl, panting and semi-conscious on the sand. 'Is she alive?'

'She is. She's goin' to stay alive too.' Billy sprawled beside them, his legs and arms stretched out as though to drink in strength from the sun. Mudurra sat erect, refusing to let weakness take him. But he accepted pomegranate juice when Juhi lugged the jug over.

Billy hefted himself up to drink. He grinned as he passed the jug to Faris. 'We did it, matey! We did it!'

Faris grinned back. Suddenly they were all grinning, except the girl on Jamila's lap. For a moment Faris felt he could face anything now — the wave, an unknown future. He looked at the others and knew they felt the same thing.

Power. They had challenged the sea. They had won. Faris lifted the jug of pomegranate juice. It was good to taste the sweetness. The whole world felt sweet.

Suddenly Susannah gave a cry. 'The doorway!'

She ran over the first bridge and tried to lift the second back to the first rock.

Faris struggled to his feet and ran over to her.

'We have to get the door back up!' She panted with the effort.

Would the doorway ever work again? Propping two pieces of driftwood up together and hanging a length of tatty hide surely could not create a doorway back to their old lives — if that's what they had ever done.

Faris looked at Susannah's face and realised that she too thought the doorway might be gone forever.

But they had to try.

David was beside him now. As they carried the second length of driftwood over the first bridge to the rocks where the door had stood, Faris saw Billy shrug and haul himself up. Mudurra followed him and the two retrieved the other bridge.

It was easy to see where the lengths of driftwood had rested, to replace them in the same position. Easy, even, for David to prop them so they leaned together, almost as if each piece remembered how it had bonded to the other. Faris heard a 'click' as the two halves met.

But he could see the beach between them. No wave, no other worlds.

Wordlessly Susannah picked up the wrinkled skin.

'How are you going to attach it?'

Susannah shoved off her shoes and socks. The socks were wet and sandy. Her feet were very white. She thrust each sock through the two holes in the top of the skin, then stood on tiptoe to tie them to the wood. She stepped back and studied the doorway.

It looked like a child's cubby house. It looked like two pieces of driftwood, propped between rocks on a beach, with a flap tied with a child's socks. It looked ridiculous.

Suddenly Susannah sank onto the sand. She began to cry, small choked sobs.

Faris glanced back at the girl Mudurra had rescued, curled on the sand with Juhi and Jamila, a thin parcel wrapped in Susannah's shawl. The girl seemed to be breathing easily now. Her eyes were still closed.

Faris kneeled by Susannah. 'I'm sorry about the door,' he said.

'We did what was right.' Her voice was small and fierce. 'We did do what was right, didn't we?'

'We did. It might still work too.'

Some of Billy's colour had come back now. 'And we got Mudurra and the girl safe, didn't we? That's what matters.'

Faris could hear the pride in his voice. 'You were a hero.' He looked over at Mudurra, sitting silently on the sand. 'And you were a warrior.'

Mudurra spoke for the first time since they had returned to the beach. 'No. Not a warrior. Yet.' He used his spear to force his body to stand up, still trembling from exhaustion. He held out his hand to Juhi.

'I am going home,' he said simply. 'Will you come through the door with me?'

'Yes,' said Juhi. She took his hand in hers.

'No!' Billy staggered towards them. 'You're mad, the both of you! What if the door don't work?'

Mudurra gave a tired grin. 'Then we will still be here. But it is time I stopped hiding, as a child.'

156

'I won't let you!' Billy stood in front of the driftwood doorway, his arms held wide. 'Remember what you're goin' back to! Remember the rocks, the fire from the sky!'

'Remember the land beyond the smoke,' said Susannah softly, from her seat on the sand. 'Your path of stars.'

'I am going back to be a warrior,' said Mudurra. 'To find my beach and the land behind it.' He met Susannah's eyes. 'A true one this time. And Juhi will come with me.'

'But she can't!' yelled Billy. 'She'll go back to her own time! You know she will!'

'I won't.' Juhi put her arm around Mudurra's waist, supporting him. 'We'll change the world together.'

'No!' shouted Billy again.

Faris grabbed his arm. 'Let them go! It's their choice!'

Billy wrenched his arm away. 'It's a stupid choice.'

'Billy,' said Susannah quietly.

His arms dropped to his sides. 'Your funeral,' he said, then gave an almost-grin. 'Nah, not a funeral. I didn't mean it like that. Good luck, matey. I hopes you get there. An' you too, girl. An' maybe the door won't work,' he added hopefully.

'I think it will.' Juhi hesitated. She left Mudurra's side, then quickly kissed Billy on the cheek. He flushed, the white skin turning red. To Faris's surprise she kissed his cheek too, then bent and hugged Susannah hard.

'We know what we're doing,' Juhi said quietly. She glanced at Mudurra, at the patched-up doorway. 'Well, perhaps we don't. But even if we can't remake the future, the land we are going to will be empty enough to find a place of peace.' She smiled at Mudurra. 'A world of our own. Sometime. Somewhere. Pray for us,' she added softly.

Mudurra reached out his hand. She clasped it again. They took three steps towards the door.

For a second they looked back. Juhi raised her hand in a small wave. Mudurra met their gazes, his face calm and resolute. They turned back to the arch.

Would the doorway work? Faris didn't know whether he hoped it would, or not. So easy to have all the choices made for you, to have to live here, unchanging, forever.

Mudurra pushed the skin aside.

For an instant the opening shone blood red in the growing shadows of the beach. A scent of burning, of sulphur, blew across the sand, the smell and mutter of another sea. Then the two figures filled the doorway. The skin flapped down again.

A cold wind drifted across the sea and sand.

Mudurra and Juhi were gone.

CHAPTER 16

The beach suddenly seemed empty. Faris shivered. Is this what it's like each time people go through the doorway? he thought. This deep and complete severing? For none of them would ever know if Juhi and Mudurra had survived that terrible sea and sky beyond the doorway.

How can we bear it?

And then he realised that they had all borne worse than this already; had left their homes, their own lands; had left all they had known to arrive here.

They had survived.

The wind still blew cold. Faris had never known a cold wind on the beach before. Somehow losing Mudurra seemed to have taken some of the warmth out of the sun.

The castaway groaned, a small thin bird-sound on the sand. She struggled to sit up. 'My sisters.' Her eyes were shadows in her dark face. Her lips were cracked and dry. The girl looked frantically about the beach. 'Where are my sisters?'

'Drink this.' Susannah held the jug of pomegranate juice to the girl's lips. The girl waved it away.

'You have to help my sisters!'

'Drink this first.'

159

The girl sipped, gulped, choked, then with an iron will seemed to control her coughing. She sipped again, more carefully, then with growing desperation and thirst. She looked up at the faces around her. 'My sisters!' she urged again. 'Are they here? Are they safe?'

'There was only you,' said Susannah quietly.

'No!' The girl lurched to her feet. She would have fallen but for Jamila's arm. 'They must still be out in the sea! Please! You must help me! We have to rescue them ...'

'You mean they were in the sea with you?'

'Yes! No!' The girl shook her head, as though to try to clear it. Her wet black plait bounced on her shoulder. 'I ... I don't know.'

Susannah and Faris shared a look of horror. He looked out at the bay again. Had there been other bodies in the water? No, he thought. We can't have missed other girls out there!

'What is the last thing you can remember?' demanded Susannah urgently.

The girl sank onto the sand again, clutching Susannah's shawl around her. 'We ... we were in a boat. It would take us to Australia. My uncle had arranged it, he sent the money to the captain.'

'Your uncle lives in Australia?'

The girl choked back a sob. She nodded. 'My uncle and my aunt. But the Australians say we cannot go to them. An aunt and uncle aren't like mother and father. So we have to hide on the boat to get there.'

Susannah stroked the girl's hand. 'We can't help you unless we know more. What place can you last remember?'

The girl looked at her, unsure. Faris kneeled down. 'You can trust Susannah,' he said. 'You can trust us all.'

Suddenly he realised what she must be seeing, their strange and varied clothes, the boys' bare scratched chests, the different-coloured skins. Why should she trust them?

'You rescued me from the sea,' she whispered. 'The young man with the black skin — he pulled me up as I sank under the water. I thought he would drown too. The other boy, the boy in red ...'

'That was Billy.' Faris leaned back so she could see Billy as well. The convict boy gave a half-salute.

'I saw you all,' she whispered. 'Saw what you did for me.' She shut her eyes, as if in pain. 'I have to trust you.'

Susannah stroked her hand again. 'I don't know how much we can help. But whatever we can do, we will.'

The girl nodded again. She gazed out to sea once more, as though hoping to see faces, a ship, even wreckage. The water was smooth again, except for the lace-edged waves.

'I am Nafeesa,' she said at last. 'My sisters and I were in the prison camp at Vavuniya.'

'An' where's that?' asked Billy, his voice attempting gentleness.

'Sri Lanka.'

'Never heard of it.'

'I have,' said Faris. 'What about your parents?'

'I think that they are dead,' said Nafeesa softly. 'I do not know. The ship's captain put us in a box, to hide us, he said. A box that stank of fish. For days, I think. We had no water. No air. Just the smell of fish.' She shuddered. 'There must have been air, or I would be dead. But not enough. We struggled, and then we were still. And then I dreamed …'

'You dreamed of Australia,' said Susannah, 'and then you were here.'

The girl looked at her in surprise. 'No. I dreamed of sky and sea and air to breathe, of room to move … Did the boat sink? Is that how I'm here?'

Susannah looked across at Billy.

'I dunno what's happenin',' he answered her unspoken question. 'No one ain't come like this before, just appearing in the sea. Each of us was in our own safe beds afore we came down to the beach.'

'Please,' Nafeesa pleaded, looking from face to face. 'We have to find my sisters!' She stared in hope as Jamila stood up. 'You'll find a rescue boat? I will do anything! My uncle will give anything! We have to get a rescue boat!'

'There is no boat. Not here. Not now. Susannah will explain it,' said Faris tiredly. 'She is good at explaining it. She has been doing it for more than eighty years.'

CHAPTER 17

The new chill wind blew stronger. They sat on the beach and ate and drank, while Jamila fed the girl small pieces of bread and cheese and sips of juice, and Susannah talked in her soft voice, with its core of iron, iron that could make the impossible seem real.

For once Billy didn't object to questions on the beach. All the rules were broken now or didn't matter. Nikko sat at Susannah's feet, making a sandcastle, as though today's triumph and tragedy had vanished.

The older boys sat in a small group, their shirts back on. They had dried quickly in the sun and wind, but Faris's shoulders felt itchy with the salt and sand.

For a while the boys just ate and drank. At last Billy said wonderingly, 'She did it, didn't she?'

'Juhi?'

'Aye. Her. She got back to his world, not hers.'

Faris nodded. Once he would have thought it a tragedy for a girl to choose a primitive existence over computers and school, the chance to go to university, a house, a car.

Now ... He shook his head. He didn't understand what Juhi had done, nor did he think she was right. But on this beach he had learned that there were many different worlds to dream of. Juhi had chosen hers. 'At least we know the doorway still works.'

Billy shrugged. Once, thought Faris, he'd have said, 'Who needs it?' or 'Better that we threw it in the sea.'

Billy had changed. We have all changed, Faris thought, even from this morning.

'How are your hands?' he asked David, suddenly remembering. 'You didn't get a splinter in them, did you?'

David smiled. 'What are hands, compared to lives?' He added, 'My hands are all right.'

Faris looked over at the girls as Jamila stood up, then helped the new girl, Nafeesa, to her feet. He stood as well, brushing the sand from his jeans.

Nafeesa looked different too. The food and drink had strengthened her. She had wrapped the shawl around her in a sort of robe. She looked fragile, so thin, but her eyes had a small private fire as she said abruptly, 'I'm going back.'

'Now? Through the door?'

Nafeesa looked a challenge at them all. 'You say the doorway will take me back to the fish box, back to my sisters? If it can do that, I have to go.'

'Not today.' Faris looked at the thin cheeks, the darkness under her eyes. Her hands still trembled, despite her determination. 'Didn't Susannah explain? You'll go back to the same moment even if you stay here a day or a week. It won't make any difference to your sisters.'

'It will to me!'

'Tomorrow,' said Susannah firmly. Faris looked at

her in surprise. He had expected Susannah to urge Nafeesa back, before whatever safe Australia she imagined tempted her to stay. But instead Susannah said: 'You'll walk through the door tomorrow, or the day after. Trust me, Nafeesa. Trust us all. You'll be stronger then. Being here will give you a chance to think. A better chance to survive what happens when you do go back.'

'It will be better for your sisters too if you are stronger, have time to plan what to do next,' said Faris. Somehow, for some reason, he didn't want this girl to go. Not yet. He wanted to know her, even knowing that any friendship must end.

For the first time Nafeesa looked unsure. 'You really think it would be better for them too?'

'Yes,' said Faris.

Billy looked towards the west. 'Sun's low in the sky,' he said. 'We need to be getting back. Look,' he said coaxingly, 'these sisters of yours, I'm betting they'll be waiting over the sand hill for you. You just walk over the sand hill and you'll see just what you dreamed.'

'And my sisters will be there?' For some reason she looked at Faris for reassurance, not Billy.

'I don't know,' Faris said honestly. 'And even if they are, they won't be real. But they'll feel real.' Then compelled by the clarity of her gaze, he added, 'For a while.'

'For as long as you want!' Billy's assurance had almost returned.

'I don't understand.' It was a demand for explanations, not a plea. 'You tell me that I will imagine my sisters safe, even when I know they are still locked in the box. How can that be?'

'I don't know.' Faris thought of the black wave, of the grey Jadda, of the warm safe Jadda beyond the sand hill. 'It just is.'

'Come on.' Susannah took Nafeesa's hand. 'You go ahead,' she said to the others. 'I'll send Nafeesa down the sand hill after you. I'll wait to make sure she gets there safely.'

'I'll stay with you.' Faris wasn't sure why he said this. He did know that he wasn't leaving this girl — or Susannah either — until he'd seen them safe into their own dream worlds. Too much had happened today, from Nafeesa's arrival to the dismantling of the doorway, to Mudurra and Juhi vanishing into the same ancient world of the volcano.

I want bean soup, he thought. I want Jadda. But he wasn't leaving till he knew the two girls were safe.

CHAPTER 18

The three of them waited on the beach side of the sand hill. The cold wind blew gusts of sand at them. They stung. One by one the others left, David first, as always.

'Play well,' Faris said to him.

David smiled. 'I'll put today into my music. Tomorrow you must come and listen.'

Tomorrow. It sounded as far off as the moon. Faris shook his head. Overload, he thought, like when you asked the computer to do too much and the program froze.

Nikko ran off after a quick hug for Susannah and a sudden, unexpected hug for Nafeesa too. 'I hope you find your sisters!' he said. Faris watched the little boy run up the sand hill, then vanish over the top.

Jamila left next, striding down to her city of women. She didn't sing her song today. Perhaps she too felt strong enough not to need it. Billy left after her.

The beach looked empty. Faris realised he had never seen it empty before. Mudurra had always been there, strong and certain. The wind ruffled the wave tops, making them tremble.

'Now it's your turn to go across the sand hill,' Susannah said quietly to Nafeesa.

'I just walk over the sand hill and my sisters will be there?' There was no belief in Nafeesa's voice. No distrust either. It was as though her mind was suddenly as tired as her body.

'Yes. And other good things too. Enjoy them. Tomorrow you can go back through the doorway. But tonight,' Susannah smiled, 'tonight be happy. Just for a while.'

Nafeesa nodded. She began to walk, her thin body swaying in Susannah's shawl, wisps of hair blowing in the wind. She looks like a queen, thought Faris, or a warrior from a movie. But she was just a girl, caring for her sisters. Which made her, he thought, a warrior indeed.

She vanished over the sand hill.

Faris was suddenly desperately curious about what sort of Australia Nafeesa might have dreamed of. A village, like Nikko's, or modern homes, like his? Her sisters laughing at an Australian buffet, perhaps, with pineapples, or maybe ... He shook his head. What foods did they eat in Sri Lanka? He had never even thought to look, never imagined that he'd ever meet someone from there. How could he understand what Nafeesa felt if he didn't even know what she liked to eat?

But he did know what she felt. They all knew. In their many different ways they had all felt it too.

'I think you can go now —' he began to say to Susannah.

He heard Nafeesa scream.

168

CHAPTER 19

He and Susannah ran up the sand hill together. Nafeesa stood at the crest, staring down, the shawl blowing against her legs in the wind.

'What is it?' called Susannah.

Nafeesa ran back towards them. 'There's nothing down there!'

'You mean just more grass and sand hills?'

'Nothing!' cried Nafeesa. 'A wall, a fence of nothing!'

'That's impossible.' Susannah grabbed Nafeesa's hand in her small one. 'Come on. You walk just a little way ahead of us. That's all it takes for your world to appear, instead of ours. We'll watch as your world appears, then follow you into it to see you safely home.'

We should have done that the first time, thought Faris.

'I can't go down! Not into that!'

'Just a little way,' urged Susannah, nudging Nafeesa over the crest of the sand hill. 'One, two, three ... now, we are coming after you. Don't be afraid.'

Faris was already following. He stopped, staring downwards. 'Susannah ...'

She pressed on. 'They'll all be waiting for you ... Faris?'

'Look.'

Susannah looked.

Nafeesa stood at the edge of — nothing. No cottages. No neat street. Just a blur of what wasn't even air or sand or even darkness. Emptiness could not be seen, yet it was there.

Faris felt cold crawl through him. Had all their worlds vanished? Had Mudurra's leaving made everything unstable? Had the others gone into nothingness too?

And then he realised what was happening. 'Susannah, there isn't a world waiting for Nafeesa. She didn't dream of one! We all dreamed of the Australia we expected. But Nafeesa just wanted to escape the box! That's why she appeared in the sea. She dreamed of nothing but the air and sea.'

'But we can't be leaving her on the beach all night!'

'We don't have to. Your world and my world will still be there. She'd be better with me,' he added. 'I'm closer to her time.'

Even as he said it, he wondered when Nafeesa had come from. Was it far in his future? How long had he been here, before he began to notice the days had passed? Even if she came from close to his own time, Nafeesa's life in Sri Lanka might have been very different from his own.

But it didn't matter. Suddenly he wanted to protect this girl, even if she was a couple of years older than him. She looked after her sisters, but who watched over her? Jadda will look after her, he thought. 'Do you like bean soup?'

Nafeesa looked at him in wonder, then nodded.

'Then come with me. I live with my grandmother. She will cook bean soup for us. You can stay with us ... just for this night.' The bean soup would not put flesh on her bones, just as the sun had never darkened Billy's convict-white skin. But it would comfort her.

Nafeesa glanced back at the beach, at the doorway leaning drunkenly between the rocks. The cliffs' shadows had already darkened the gold of the sand. Faris had never stayed so late on the beach before.

An empty beach, he thought. The beach that Mudurra dreamed of. But now Mudurra had gone.

'One night,' he said. One night, with bean soup and Jadda.

He could see when Nafeesa decided to stay. The nothingness took form, houses emerged and orange trees and the quiet munching shapes of kangaroos.

His world. His safe Australia.

Faris took her hand. He had never held a young woman's hand before. Susannah was a little girl and didn't count. 'Come on,' he said.

They walked down the sand hill together. Susannah watched them go.

CHAPTER 20

The storm came swiftly, out of the midnight sky.

Faris had been dreaming. Or maybe it was a memory, dressed in sleep. His mother had been there, so he must have been young, before he'd gone to school even. She wore bracelets of gold with small red stones. Were they the family bracelets Jadda had sold? She laughed as she held him on her knee.

His father was there too, not the man with a bloody jacket and worried eyes, but a young man who smiled at his wife and son. 'Now repeat after me,' he said to baby Faris. 'This bone is the fibula. This is the tibia. These are the phalanges ...'

His mother laughed again. 'Darling, he is much too young to learn anatomy.'

The young father grinned. 'Are you saying our son is not a genius? He'll remember this, won't you, Faris?'

And Faris had, even if it needed a dream to bring the memory back. For a moment he tried not to wake, to keep the memory. Even when he knew he was awake, it didn't make him sad.

It should have, for those three were gone, the laughing woman, the little boy, the young and happy father. But somehow remembering them had made him realise that life changed.

Life needs to change, he thought. But it doesn't here.

And then he realised change had come here too.

Thunder muttered above the house. He had never heard a storm here before. Who would want to hear thunder? Rain kicked at the window, like a bully trying to get in.

His bedroom door opened. 'Faris?' It was Jadda, a Jadda with worry behind her smile. 'Faris, it's just thunder. Go back to sleep.'

Another memory pierced him. A roaring from the sky, a small boy hiding his head under the blanket, Jadda coming in to comfort him, Jadda saying exactly what she had said just now.

But it hadn't been thunder then. It had been bombs and guns. And the Jadda he saw now was the memory of that Jadda.

He had known his life here wasn't real. Not really real. But now even the ghost of reality seemed stripped away.

He said, 'Jadda?'

She looked at him. 'I love you, Faris.'

'I love you too,' he said. For it was true. He loved this Jadda, even if she was a memory. And the Jadda of his memory loved him too.

'Would you like me to sing to you?'

It was what Jadda had asked him as a little boy, scared of the bombs, the rumble of tanks, the chatter that might have been monkeys on TV, or distant guns. He had said 'yes' then. But this time he shook his head. 'No. I'm all right.'

Someone moved in the hall. He brushed past Jadda. 'Nafeesa? Where are you going?'

The girl paused. She wore the clothes Jadda had found for her earlier this evening, before she had fed her bean soup, shown her the bright bedroom with its lace-covered bed, its clean tiles on the floor and rich carpets. Somehow Jadda's long dress had fitted Nafeesa perfectly, the scarf gold and blue against the darkness of her hair.

And Jadda was no longer there. It was just the two of them, him and Nafeesa, in the bare corridor with closed doors.

'It's just a storm,' said Faris. 'No need to worry.' Even as he said it, his uneasiness grew.

'I'm sorry. I left you a note. I didn't want to wake you. But I can't stay here any longer. I have to get back to my sisters.'

'Not in the storm. Not at night. Nafeesa, you still don't understand. You can go back any time —'

'I am going now!' She met his eyes. 'You think I can sleep in a soft bed when my sisters lie in a box that smells of fish?'

He had left Jadda under the black wave. Had told himself it made no difference.

Nafeesa was right. It mattered.

The knowledge rocked him, as though the wave had already hit. He shook his head to clear it. 'Not tonight.' Would the beach even be there at night? he wondered. The beach was a place of daylight, of sunlit sand and laughter. None of them had ever been on the beach at night.

Except Mudurra, looking at his avenue of stars.

'I'm going to go through the door too,' Faris said. 'Tomorrow, as soon as it is light.'

'Now,' she insisted. She held out her hand. He had held his mother's hands, and Jadda's. Nafeesa's were warm and strong like theirs, but smaller. Her hair smelled of orange blossom, as familiar as if he had known her all his life.

He couldn't leave without saying goodbye to Susannah, to Billy and the others. Not without telling them that Susannah was right, that Nafeesa was right. Real was what you had been given, what you had to live, taking it with courage, doing the best you could do, even when life became unendurably hard.

If the beach wasn't there till daylight, he would wait on the sand hill with Nafeesa till it came back. And if it was there — if Nafeesa went through the doorway in the darkness — he would wait on the beach until the others came in the morning, take the time to say goodbye to them.

But he had to go.

He turned, and Jadda was there again. 'We're going to live,' he told her. 'The wave will come down on us, but we'll swim up to the surface. We'll find something that floats ...' He stopped, unable to envisage exactly how they might survive.

The words didn't matter. For Jadda was smiling at him, as though she knew he had made the right decision, because this was the right thing to do.

'I love you,' he whispered again and saw Jadda smile.

He walked with Nafeesa along the silent corridor and out into the rain.

CHAPTER 21

The kangaroos had vanished. St Kangarou, he thought. The houses on either side of the street were dark. But the streetlights shone above them, outlining the road. The wind buffeted them. Rain dripped from their faces.

Nafeesa's hand was still in his.

He glanced down. His pyjamas had vanished. So had the new jeans and joggers too. He wore his old clothes, stained and dull from the months in Indonesia. He could smell their sour scent, over the salt and sea.

Nafeesa's clothes were grey and shapeless again. They stank of fish.

The road turned and there was the sand hill, tall but glowing with an almost phosphorescent shine. They began to climb, the rain lashing at their faces. He had never known the sand hill wet before, but now the sand squished under his feet. At last they reached the top. Faris looked down.

Waves tore at the golden beach. For a terrified moment he thought they had already washed away the driftwood doorway. Then he saw that it was still there. The rocks had protected it as the waves sucked and tore at the shore. But even as he looked, the doorway shuddered in the water.

Had they loosened the doorway when they took it apart? Had Mudurra dreamed the doorway? Dreamed the beach? Was the storm here because Mudurra had left? Was Mudurra's dream fading as his real world took over?

The reason didn't matter now. If the door was swept away by the storm, they would be trapped here, every one of them.

And what if others came, others who had sought refuge, and become lost on their way to Australia? They too would be trapped if the doorway was gone, with no way to fight their way back to what was real.

'No!' Nafeesa let go of his hand. She ran, holding up her skirt, ignoring the rain, the wind, the frothy waves that crashed around her ankles. He waited for her to go through the doorway. Instead she grasped one of the driftwood posts.

Desperate, grieving, she was trying to protect the doorway — to give them all a chance to leave too. Even as he looked, the door lurched again, as though letting the sea claim it.

Could he and Nafeesa hold the doorway in place until the storm died down, till daylight came, and the others arrived at the beach?

He didn't know.

He turned and looked back to his street. The clean houses, the rose gardens had disappeared. There was only darkness, only the storm.

'Billy!' he yelled, throwing his voice out into the darkness. 'Susannah! Jamila! David! Help us! Please,

please help us! The doorway is washing out to sea! Please, help us now!'

The wind ate his words. He had only one choice left now.

He turned again and ran down to the beach, waded through the rising tide and grabbed the other side of the doorway.

CHAPTER 22

The waves rose around his knees, sucking and sobbing. Or was that him crying into the night? The water smelled of sea monsters, of every fear he'd ever had.

He looked across at Nafeesa and saw tears on her face too. But he also saw determination. A wave splashed high, the foam hitting his face. The rough timber between his hands shifted, just a little. He wedged his feet between the rocks.

Another wave. Another. They rose no higher now, but they were stronger.

The timber moved again, twisting in his fingers. Each wave inched the doorway just slightly towards the sea.

'Nafeesa?' His voice was a gasp in the wind. 'What was in the note you left me?' He would never read it now.

She said nothing. He thought she hadn't heard him, or perhaps had no strength to spare to answer. Then she said, 'It was easier to say on paper. I am embarrassed.'

'Tell me.'

'I said thank you.' Her voice was almost lost in the mutter of the sea. 'The captain took us on the ship for money. My uncle sent the money because it is his duty. You are the only person who helped me because I am me.'

'Now you helped us.' Nafeesa could have gone straight through the doorway. But she stood here, fighting the waves with him. A wave splashed hard against him, scattering salt foam on his face. It sucked back, dragging the doorframe with it. He pushed as hard as he could, digging his feet into the sand, feeling the water erode it from underneath him.

They couldn't do it. A boy and a girl could never hold the doorframe against the storm. He glanced at Nafeesa. She gripped the post in both thin hands. He opened his mouth to tell her to go through the doorway now, while she could, to find her sisters, to leave him here to explain what had happened to his friends.

A voice yelled behind him. Suddenly Susannah was flying down the sand hill, her shawl flapping in the wind.

'The doorway is going!' he screamed.

Once again the wind whipped away his words. But somehow Susannah heard them, just as she must have heard his terrified scream from up on the hill. She splashed through the water. Her small hands grasped the doorframe next to his as other figures tumbled through the darkness: David in striped pyjamas, holding Nikko by the hand; Jamila in a long blue dress and scarf, dashing through the storm as though she gloried in the battle.

They clustered about the doorframe, holding it, heaving at it with their bones.

The timbers inched again, another fraction towards the sea.

'Just let it go!'

Billy waded towards them, his face white. Faris realised that the clouds had gone. Above them an avenue of stars led to the sea, the trail in the sky that Mudurra had spoken of.

'We don't need no door!' Billy shouted above the crash of waves.

'Billy, please.' Susannah stretched out one of her hands, the other clutching the doorframe. 'We can't hold the door without you. Please, Billy!'

'You're a fool!'

'A fool I may be! But without this doorway, we'll all be in prison, just like you have been. Can you do that to us, Billy Higgs?'

Another wave swept in, higher than the rest. Faris felt the water at his shoulder. The doorframe moved again.

'Billy!' There was a note in Susannah's voice he had never heard before. She loves him, he thought. Susannah loves Billy. And then he recognised the tone more clearly.

It was Jadda's tone when she spoke to him. It was a mother's love, and a grandmother's, even though it was spoken by a child.

And suddenly Billy was beside them, his strength with theirs. They stood there, all of them together, holding the doorframe, letting the waves batter them.

Holding fast.

CHAPTER 23

Dawn came like a grey kitten, peering up above the sea. The grey grew stronger, became light. The last wisps of cloud faded to blue.

The beach was clean and gold again.

Faris felt relief creep through his mind. Mudurra might be gone, but the beach was back again. Although it still seemed empty, not as bright as before. But at least it still existed.

They sprawled exhausted on the sand. Susannah held Nikko on her lap. At last Nafeesa sat up and brushed the sand from her thin face and hands. She stared at them, tumbled and wave torn. 'Thank you,' she said. 'I am going now. I ... I think you should go too,' she added. 'Every one of you.'

'She's right.' To Faris's surprise it was Billy's voice. 'I reckon that door's a goner. It'll be washed away in tonight's tide, or the next one. We can't hold it in place forever. If any of you wants to go, it'd better be now.'

'Go back to what?' David's voice was bitter.

'I want to grow tall.' Faris looked at Nikko in surprise. He hadn't thought the little boy understood what was happening. Now Nikko looked at them all, small and solemn. He knows, thought Faris.

183

'My nonna said I would grow tall in Australia,' said Nikko. 'So tall I would have to bend my head to come through the door, just like my uncles. My mother measures me every night against the wall. But I don't grow at all.' Nikko looked wistfully at Susannah. 'If I go through there, will I grow tall?'

'Yes.' Susannah stroked his face softly.

Jamila clenched her fists. 'I want to taste ice-cream. My grandmother read me a book that talked about ice-cream. I want ... I want the bad things too! How will things like that change if people don't fight them?' She held her chin high. 'I will be a fighter, but not with guns or knives. If I stay here, the Taliban man on my boat will get to Australia. There will be no one to say, "This man's papers are false. Don't trust him." We thought that we needed Australia. But maybe Australia needs us too. My grandmother stood up for what she believed in. They killed her. I will not let them kill me. I won't hide forever in a dream.'

'And you'll get better from your fever,' Faris said to Susannah.

She smiled at him. 'You don't have to convince me, boyo. Once I've got all you through the door, I'll be off to my real family like Murphy's goat after the cabbages. I'll dance my way to Australia. David?'

David looked at his hands, his long perfect fingers that had been scarred and deformed in his other life. 'There is no life beyond the door for me,' he said flatly. 'No family. No music. What have I got to look forward to?'

'Families can be made. And music too.' Jamila took David's hands in hers. 'What kept you alive in the concentration camp, David? Even when your hands were scarred? What seed of hope was deep inside you?'

He looked at her in shock. 'I heard a bird,' he whispered. 'A nightingale. I thought, even here, there is music in the world.'

'Go and find the music of new birds singing, of the wind in the trees,' said Jamila softly. 'Music you've never dreamed of, not made by man at all. Write music, if you can't play it. Listen to the wonder of it all. Find your aunt in Australia, and a new family. One day find a woman who loves you too.'

'How could a woman love a man with hands that are scarred and twisted?'

'You are more than your hands,' said Jamila. 'I will still be a child when you are an old, old man. You cannot wait your life for me. But I will tell you this, David Weisengarten. If you were a man and I a woman, we would have children and I would make you glad.'

Suddenly David laughed. It was a strange laugh, but a laugh nonetheless. 'You're going through the doorway now?'

Jamila held her head high. 'Yes. I am a daughter of brave mothers and brave fathers too. I will not die. It is time to find my courage. And when I come to Australia, I'll expect to see you there, an old man who will take me to concerts and explain the music, who will ask me to dinner with his grandchildren, who will tell me of the good life carved by a boy who had nothing but courage and love.'

David took her hand and kissed it. 'The brave daughter of brave mothers may need help in a new land. If — when — I am an old man in Australia, I will find you and help you. I promise.'

'We have done the impossible,' Susannah said quietly. 'All of us here. We found a refuge in our dreams. Now it is time to make our dreams real.'

Nikko looked uncertain suddenly. 'I ... I don't want to go alone,' he said in a small voice. He turned to Susannah. 'I can come with you, can't I?'

'Of course you can.' Susannah took his hand.

Faris stared at her. 'You can't take Nikko to your time!'

'Why not? Juhi went with Mudurra.'

'But Nikko can't just appear on your ship ...'

'My mother has sixteen children,' said Susannah calmly, 'and only fourteen of them hers. There's always room for another.'

One who speaks Greek? thought Faris. But perhaps Susannah was right. Nikko was in danger of drowning if he went back to his own time. Better to appear speaking a strange language than be alone in the sea.

Suddenly Faris realised that he would miss his friends more than the beach, more than his bright bedroom, more than his dreams.

And yet it was time to go.

CHAPTER 24

They formed a line. There was no need, but for some reason the ceremony seemed right. Susannah smiled at Faris from her spot next to Billy at the end of the line. Of all of them, hers was the only face that smiled, that shone with faith and confidence.

Nafeesa was first. She looked back at Faris over the heads of Jamila and David. 'I'll look for you,' she said. 'I'll find you too. I'll say thank you properly.'

Faris nodded, unable to speak. Billy was from nearly two hundred years before his time. How far in his future was Nafeesa's life? Would he be an old man too when she found him?

Was it even possible to find each other once they'd passed through the door?

'Goodbye. And thank you. Thank you all.' Nafeesa gave Faris one last long look, then turned and pushed aside the tattered skin. It was sodden and heavy, water splattered.

Would the doorway still work? Perhaps the sea had tried to take it because it had already lost its power. Would Nafeesa step only to the other side of this strange, shabby version of a doorframe?

Then for an instant he saw bodies, darkness; smelled fear and fish.

The skin fell back. Nafeesa was gone.

Jamila shivered, the horror of what she had seen etched on her face. Then she forced herself to give them all a final smile. 'May Allah bless you all with all His unseen blessings,' she whispered. 'May He bless all the children of mankind.'

She stepped over to the doorway and pushed at the skin. The world beyond was dark, with the steady swish of waves — and pierced by a woman's scream. For an instant they heard Jamila yell. But the yell was of determination, not of terror.

David followed her quickly, so quickly Faris wondered if perhaps he was trying to share Jamila's world, as Juhi had with Mudurra. But if so, he was too late. For David stepped into a world of thin white faces, bare benches that served as beds, a pile of what might be bodies.

Then that too vanished as the skin fell down.

Faris was glad Nafeesa had gone first. Each scene was like a blow.

Four of them left.

'Now you,' Susannah said to Billy.

'Ladies go first,' he said.

'You've learned that at least,' said Susannah. 'Good manners for a convict lad. Now through the door with you.'

Billy smiled. 'You know that I'm not going.'

Faris stared at him. 'You can't stay here by yourself!'

'Why not? Mudurra did.'

Faris shook his head. How long had Mudurra really been alone? If time had no meaning here, if it shifted and washed about like the waves, perhaps Mudurra had dreamed away the time.

But Billy, alone here? Billy, with no game on the sand, no gang to boss? Could Billy's fine dreamed-of farm, his servants and Mrs Bonnet be enough to keep him from loneliness, once all of them had gone? Could he dream hard enough to keep the beach real, without Mudurra?

'You've got lives ahead of you. I'm convict scum,' said Billy.

'No,' said Faris. 'You're the best of us!'

The big boy stared.

'You saved Nafeesa and Mudurra. You held the doorway. You've looked after us all, you and Susannah.'

'She's the brave one.'

'You both are.'

'You are the best and bravest I have ever known, Billy Higgs.' Susannah's voice was firm. 'So you go through there. You give that blaggard with his sharpened spoon a punch on the snout, then another one from me as well. You serve your seven years. What's seven years after the time you've spent here? Because I'm thinking that in two times seven, or three maybe, you'll be the finest gentleman in the land, with the biggest farm in all of New South Wales.'

'Not me.' But Billy's eyes had hope. 'You ain't leaving unless I go, are you?' he added.

Susannah shook her head. 'I'll stay here till the sea washes every grain of sand away. I'm not going till you step through that door too.'

'Well then, I better go. For you.'

Faris gazed at them. He knew that Susannah loved Billy, loved them all. But he hadn't known till that moment how much Billy loved Susannah.

Billy would go through the doorway for her. Perhaps it would be for her sake, not just his own, that he would survive, make good, so the long years Susannah had spent watching on the sand hill would have been worth it.

Billy bent and kissed Susannah's cheek. He patted Nikko on the head, then clapped Faris on the back. 'Live good, the three of youse,' he said. He stepped through the door.

Darkness filled the doorway, darker than Faris had ever known, and the stench of human filth. What have we sent Billy to? thought Faris. And then, What am *I* going to now?

'Come on.' Susannah smiled down at Nikko. 'Remember what I said? Through there I'll be sick in my bunk, but you're not to be scared. You're to tell the lady that she's your mam now, and wait for me to get better. You understand?'

'I say, "You are my mam."'

'That's it.' Susannah tightened her grip on Nikko's small hand.

'You trust me to go through? Not to try to stay here?' asked Faris.

'Oh, yes. I trust you,' said Susannah. 'Didn't we all trust each other with our futures, here last night? God be with you,' she whispered quickly and stepped forwards. The skin swept up and back, leaving a whisper of what might have been prayers.

He was alone.

CHAPTER 25

He could sit here on the beach, Faris realised. Just sit. Listen to the waves and feel the peace.

Wait a breath and then another before he faced the wave. Sit here forever, as the sun slid across the sky. Somehow he knew he'd never starve, not here, even if he never made another visit to the house beyond the sand hill. The food he had eaten here had tasted good. It hadn't fed him. You can't starve when you live among your dreams.

One more look at the bright blue sky, the clear line of the horizon, the golden sand, the tumbling froth of waves, innocent and obedient as though they had never torn at the doorframe and its protectors last night.

Would he remember how they had faced the waves, and won, once he went through the door? Would he remember Susannah's wisdom, Jamila's strength, Billy's protectiveness, Nikko's laugh? The glory of David's music, Juhi's passion for a land that was free of hate, Mudurra's courage?

Yes, he thought. I will remember.

It was time to go.

'Goodbye,' he said to the beach and to the memory of his friends.

I won't forget, he thought. And I will live!

He stepped through the doorway.

CHAPTER 26

For a moment there was nothing, no space, no time. Only hope and the lingering warmth of the sand on his feet.

Then that too was gone.

Suddenly water filled his mouth: bitter, salty. His body hurt, as if a giant hand had swatted him. He choked, sinking, his hands flailing despite the pain. He could see bubbles above him, the dark green of water below.

Where was Jadda? Was she lost in the deep of the ocean too?

'No!' It wasn't a cry, but a promise. He moved his hands purposefully now, propelling himself up, up, up, till suddenly the sea burst open and there was air and light.

'Jadda!' he screamed, pushing with his feet and legs to keep his head above the water, instinctively moving as he had seen Mudurra do out in the sea as he'd hauled Nafeesa to safety ...

Waves slopped against him — not monsters now, but large enough to batter him and to fill his mouth with salty water. He gulped air in the brief gaps when his face was clear, frantically gazing around him.

A man shouted a name, above the noise of water. A

voice cried, 'Pray for us!' And then the sea was silent as the wrecked and wretched used their strength to cling to life. A tangle of clothes and feet that had already become a body floated near him, part of the sea's debris and not a living person. It was as though the beach he'd left had never been.

They'd fought the sea there and won. He wouldn't give up now. I'll beat you, he told the ocean. Somewhere there is a real beach, a real Australia. All I have to do to find it is to live.

'Jadda!' he shouted again. It was impossible to see above the slapping waves.

'Faris!' The word was choked, desperate. He managed to force his body part of the way around. There was Jadda, her hand on one of the big kerosene tins that had been filled with water. But this one floated under her hand.

It must be empty, he thought, remembering how Mudurra's water bladders had floated, even as Jadda pushed the empty tin towards him.

He grasped it.

For a second the tin sank under his added weight, so he thought it couldn't support them both. But it stayed only a little way below the splashing, slapping surface, enough to keep them both floating. All around them bits of wood and rag floated. From somewhere, too far beyond the white-tipped waves to see, he heard the sound of thrashing arms or legs, a sudden harsh wail of anguish, grief, pain or terror.

Jadda called out something above the noise of water. He thought she was asking if he was all right, but the sea slaps sucked her words away. He tried to nod at her, to say he wasn't hurt.

He glanced up at the sky. A grey sky still: too grey — not just cloud, but the coming night.

He tried not to think of the water growing dark about them, or of sharks, drawn by the smell of blood. Was it worse to be taken by an invisible shark, or to catch a glimpse before it lunged at you? Did a shark's bite kill you straight away?

He didn't know.

How long could they float here? Already his arms screamed with the strain of clinging to the container; his legs seemed too big, swollen with kicking to help them stay afloat. How long would Jadda's strength last?

He looked at her and then he knew: Jadda would hold on for his sake. Love would give as much strength as she needed.

Jadda shouted again. Once more he tried to answer her.

And then he understood. Jadda was looking at something behind his head.

It was a ship.

CHAPTER 27

The ship was grey, like sky and sea. Men moved on the deck. All at once something orange splashed into the ocean next to Faris. A rock, he thought, remembering how Mei Ling's ship had met pirates.

This was no rescue ship! They were pirates, trying to kill every witness ...

But even as he thought it, he realised that there was no reason for pirates to kill survivors from a shipwreck — if there had been anything on board worth stealing it was gone now, with the boat.

The rock hadn't sunk. It floated a few metres away. A lifebuoy? he thought in confusion. He pushed himself across to it, leaving the air-filled tin to Jadda, then splashed back to her, so they could both keep a hand each on the tin and one on the buoy, almost making their own boat, nearly stable in the waves.

For the first time he thought that they might live.

Time stretched. He was too weak now to keep the ship in sight as he and Jadda were washed by waves and currents. The world was water, numbness beyond pain. Then at last, after what seemed a century of hoping, a lifetime of gulping salt, a rubber boat bobbed next to them.

A man reached for him, a big man in what looked like a uniform. Faris shook his head. He tried to tell them to rescue Jadda first, but the salt had frozen his throat and swollen his mouth. He saw Jadda was gesturing to him. He let the man take him, grabbing his shirt and hauling him headfirst into the shallow water at the bottom of the rubber boat, knowing that Jadda would wait — would always wait — till he was safe.

He took a breath, and then another, drawing in strength to struggle to his knees, to look around as the two men dragged Jadda into the rubber boat too, her clothes and hair grey in the grey light and water, everything grey, except her white face.

Her eyes found him as they laid her down.

He tried to stand. His legs wouldn't obey. He crawled over to Jadda instead, across the rubber floor of the boat. Her lips were blue, the area around them blue too. But she smiled when she saw him. She lifted a weak hand and stroked his wet hair.

He lay beside her for a minute or perhaps a year, perhaps eternity. If time had no place on the beach, then it had too many places here.

Voices yelled, in English.

'Any more alive, do you think?'

'Don't think so.'

Faris tried not to think of the other faces on the boat, of the voice that had called 'pray for us'.

One man spoke into what looked like a large mobile phone. Faris caught only the tail end of the words: '... you keep on here. These two need the medic ... Over and out.'

An engine noise, a different sound from the engine of the boat from Indonesia. The rubber boat moved in a different way now, across the waves instead of bobbing on them. One of the voices asked, 'Madam, do you speak English?'

A face peered down. Jadda muttered something, too low to hear.

Faris struggled to sit up. Strong hands helped him. 'She is an English teacher. We speak English well.' His voice sounded like the sea had washed most of it away.

The man gave an almost-smile. 'You do indeed, mate. You OK sitting there? We'll get a blanket around you. And one for your mother too.'

'She is my grandmother,' said Faris. 'My mother is dead.'

The man glanced out at the wreckage-strewn sea. 'I'm sorry. We'll try to find —'

'She died years ago,' said Faris. He hesitated. 'Please, are we going to Australia?'

The man's face seemed to lose expression. 'To Christmas Island. Maybe after that, to Australia.'

His papers! Faris felt under his shirt. They were still there, tied in their plastic bags. He could only hope that the water hadn't soaked them.

The man in uniform helped Faris lift Jadda so she could sit too. Suddenly there were blankets around them, strange shiny blankets, and mugs of something hot and sweet. He sipped his, but Jadda's mug dropped, her hands shaking too much to hold it. Faris held his mug to her mouth while she tried to sip it.

Thunder growled. The storm had circled back. A wave slopped into the rubber boat. Jadda gave a short sharp cry. But their boat had nearly reached the big ship now.

Faris looked at the crew. Had these men risked their lives, riding in this rubber boat on a storm-boiled sea to save them? Or had they stayed away, till the storm was gone and it was safe? Were they good men trying to help, or men who just did their job? He didn't know. Perhaps it didn't matter. But deep down he knew it did. He wanted the gift of life to come from heroes.

He shut his eyes briefly. There was too much to think about. Too much to feel. The refuge he had known was still with him, along with Susannah and Nikko, Jamila, Nafeesa, Billy, David, Mudurra and Juhi, but it was fading, like the storm. A storm was hard and real, and then it was gone, and the beach felt like that too.

It couldn't have been real.

It was the realest thing that he had ever known.

'Faris,' whispered Jadda. He was shocked at how old she looked. The grandmother he had been seeing had been younger, her face unlined and happy, not this ghost-faced Jadda with shadowed eyes.

He put his arm around her. 'Yes?' She felt as light as Nafeesa, even in her wet clothes.

Her voice was just a breath. 'Tell the officials about your father. Who he is, why we had to leave. Show them your papers. Tell them how old you are.'

He was scared by the blue around her lips. 'Yes. I'll tell them. Rest now. We're safe.'

He didn't know if that was true. But somehow now it was his job to look after Jadda, not hers to look after him.

'Such a sweet boy,' whispered Jadda. 'He used to sing to me, his own songs, *lalalala*. I thought, he will be a musician. But when it mattered, he was strong.'

She was talking about his father, Faris realised. 'Hush,' he said softly, under the engine's noise. 'Lean on me. We're nearly there.'

He didn't mean the ship, though it was there too, a grey wall above them. He meant safety. A real refuge, not the one where he had been. A new life, a real one, for them both.

A strange sling thing descended. The man who had spoken to them kneeled down by Jadda. 'Madam, we need to ...'

She gave a sudden cry. For a terrible second Faris thought the man had stabbed her. He looked for a knife, then saw the alarm on the man's face. The man called out something unintelligible to someone on the ship above.

Jadda slumped to the boat's rubber floor. Her body twitched.

Faris clasped her to him. 'Jadda! What's wrong ...?'

She looked at him, her face unmoving, her eyes helpless. Her lips moved. He bent to try to hear the words, but there was no breath behind them. He thought he heard 'love'.

Her body jerked once more, as though a giant had straightened her limbs. Her eyes stared up. Her mouth fell open.

'Jadda! We are nearly there!'

But Jadda didn't move.

CHAPTER 28

Christmas Island Detention Centre, Australia

The room was small. The desk was neat. The woman on the other side looked tired. Beyond this room were more rooms. But mostly there were walls and fences, real ones and legal ones, to keep him and the other detainees from Australia.

He hadn't understood, on the sagging boat on its way here, how much Australia didn't want him.

But he had nowhere else to go.

He had spent his time in this place lying on his bed, staring at the blank wall, trying to make his mind blank too, trying not to think of the lives that he had lost, of Jadda, or Susannah and Billy, Nafeesa and Jamila, David his face lost and intent as he played his violin. He had given them all up, the golden beach and the laughing waves, the comfort of Jadda's arms. He had given them all up, for this.

Each time Faris remembered them he forced his mind away.

His life on the beach could not have happened. Didn't happen. And if it had, then it was gone, just as

Jadda was gone. This was his world now. There was no door to step through this time.

You breathed in fear, in detention. Fear of being sent back to wherever you had come from. Fear that no one would want you, that you would spend your life behind barbed wire. Fear of other inmates sometimes. Anger was so sharp you could almost touch it. Angry men shouted and shoved; men sat unmoving on their beds, their eyes down, but when they looked up you could not bear the bitterness in their eyes. Children yelled, turning their terror into anger too. But mostly they just waited. They were good at waiting. These children had waited most of their lives.

Faris was so lonely it was almost as if he wasn't there. Everyone in the camp was in the same place, but none shared his past, or future. No one knew him. Dimly he knew he would have to battle laws he didn't know anything about before Australia would allow him to make a new existence.

He was supposed to call someone, to say he had arrived in Australia — the 'alive' call so the owner of the boat would get his money. But he had no number to ring.

Days had passed. Weeks or months, perhaps, as someone, somewhere, checked out the papers that had survived the journey and his story. Some of the inmates said that you had to wait years here or in some other camp. Faris didn't count the time. It simply passed. In a strange way the beach had been more vivid than real life.

This was not the Australia he had dreamed of. But it was all he had.

The woman with tired eyes tapped notes into her laptop. Faris thought of Jadda and forced himself to speak, referring the woman again to his papers. 'I am thirteen, just like my birth certificate says, and the report from my school. No, I have no family, except for my father. He lives in Sydney. He is a good man, a doctor ...'

It almost felt like a lie. The man who waited for him didn't seem like a father. A father didn't abandon you for years. Once again Faris felt the helpless terror of that night his father had vanished.

What had his father done to bring this upon his son? Why had he done it? How could any man sacrifice his family like that?

Now — perhaps — he could ask him.

At last the woman met his eyes. She smiled and nodded. Faris felt that she was glad that she could nod, not shake her head. Had an exception been made for him, because he had lost his grandmother, because he had a father who was in Australia? He didn't know the rules. It didn't matter. He had a classification now: he was an unaccompanied minor. A child.

He wasn't a child. Not any more. But at least this was the first step to staying in Australia.

A plane trip. Below him, briefly, stretched long beaches, a sea almost the colour of the one he'd known, and then the grey of clouds. He was as unsubstantial as the clouds, a package to be delivered.

An airport, like every other airport. He sat in a chair bolted to other chairs with a woman to look after him, as though he had not crossed the world, fought an ocean, as though a woman was needed to protect him now. The woman was kind, the sort of practised kindness that said: you are a stranger. Soon you will leave and another will take your place, and I will give him the same smile that I give you.

Another plane trip, a glimpse of long white beach and deep blue sea; then more clouds then into darkness broken by the muttering of a movie on the screen above, too blurred to see; food in a plastic tray and then an iceblock, its coldness suddenly real, the first thing he had really tasted since the bitterness of the ocean.

The plane dropped slowly towards the lights of Sydney. He looked out the window and saw darkness that must be the sea, then the plane bumped down onto the ground.

I should be excited, Faris thought. He wasn't.

He walked along the big plastic tube from the plane, looking at the waiting faces.

A man stepped forwards. A tired thin man, with short hair that was grey as well as black, a smooth shaved face and shadowed eyes. A stranger. But this stranger was his father.

Faris stared at him. Why did you leave us? he thought. Why did you bring all this upon us?

The stranger hesitated, then reached out his arms. Faris participated in the hug. He thought they were both relieved when it was over.

They sat side by side on the bus as it bumped through tunnels of light and dark. He thought he saw tears glint on the man's face, but when he looked again they were gone. It was a reflection, he thought, from the glass.

'Soon be there,' said the man. He spoke English, as he had since they had met. Faris didn't know if his father always spoke English now, or just didn't want to draw attention by speaking another language. Faris understood the need to be discreet. He had lived with it ever since his father was taken. This was not the time to talk of Jadda either, or what had happened years before.

The man hesitated again. 'I am afraid the flat is small. Only one bedroom. But the school is only a few streets away.'

'Is the beach near too?'

The man looked startled. 'A beach? No. We're on the wrong side of Sydney. An hour away by bus. Two hours maybe.'

The bus stopped. They walked along a street and round a corner, then up concrete stairs that smelled of garbage.

The flat smelled of garbage too, but it was clean. There was not much in it: an old TV set, the smallest Faris had ever seen. A flimsy table, two chairs, a fridge like a small box. A bedroom, with two small beds on either side.

'Take whichever bed you like,' said the man, and suddenly, even though the man was a stranger, Faris wanted to cry for him, because all he had to offer was a choice of beds.

Faris put his small bag on the nearest bed. He waited for the man to talk of Jadda, to speak of home. Instead the man said: 'Faris, I'm sorry, I need to go to work.'

'At the hospital?'

The man's face was carefully blank. 'I drive a taxi here. I need to pass examinations to practise again as a doctor. Until I do ...' He paused, then said again, 'I'm sorry. I wanted to be here on your first night, but one of the other drivers is sick and ...' He shrugged. 'I must take what work I can. Is there anything you want before I go?'

I want Jadda, thought Faris. I want my real life, our house, my old school. I want my friends! 'What did you do?' he asked abruptly.

The man stared, not understanding.

'Why did the police take you away? What secrets did you hide from us?'

The man sat on the other bed. He clasped his hands together. Faris saw them shaking. 'I kept no secrets from you. Or your grandmother.'

'Then why did they take you? Was it a mistake?'

'No. Or partly.' His father looked at his hands. 'That day. That terrible day. The traffic was bad. A demonstration. The driver let me off three blocks from the hospital. It was quicker to walk than be driven. I was careful to stay well away from the demonstration. I heard shots and screams.'

His father hesitated. 'One block from the hospital a man lay in a doorway. He had been shot through the temporal lobe, the forehead. The bullet must have missed the brain. He was still alive. He stared at me, blood around his head.'

The man who was his father met Faris's eyes. 'I am a doctor. Even here, where I drive taxis, I am still a doctor. I was one that day too. I kneeled to help him. Another man called to me to bring him inside. And then another yelled to run, run, the soldiers were coming.

'I left him. Even though I am a doctor, I left my patient. I ran to the hospital. But there was blood on my jacket. I took it off, put on my white coat. But others had seen it. I saw it on their faces. I knew one, at least, would call the police.

'I did my rounds. I went home. I told Jadda.' He shrugged. 'You know the rest. Jadda sent you out. We waited for the police to come. Jadda didn't tell you of this?'

Faris shook his head. 'She said I should know nothing, so I could say I knew nothing, if I was asked. So it was all a mistake?'

His father looked at him steadily. 'I should have been at that demonstration. I should have had the courage to say: "These things must change." But if I had known more, I might have told the police when they beat me, might have led them as they hoped to other rebels when they let me out. So perhaps it is best that I did not protest that day, or any other. But I am sorry. So sorry to have brought you to this.'

Did he mean to this small poor room? Or to Jadda's death, the years of fear?

Faris said nothing. The man who was his father waited for him to speak. 'It's all right,' he said at last.

'I ... I am glad to see you. You have grown so tall. Your English is so good too.' The man tried a smile. 'You will have no trouble at school, I think.'

Faris thought of the wave, of the battle with his friends to keep the doorway open, of Jadda dying as she breathed the word 'love'. No, school would be no trouble, after that.

Nothing here matters, he thought.

Yet it was real. And it was all he had.

CHAPTER 29

Gibber's Creek, Australia, three years later

His school shirt was too tight. Faris stared at himself in the mirror. In his first two years in Australia he had hardly grown at all. Now he was sixteen it seemed as if his body had finally accepted he was safe and could spare the energy to grow.

It had been a good year. The only year in his life so far that he could say, 'This has been good.'

He tried to forget his first year in Australia. It was easy to forget. Every few weeks there had been change, too much for his shocked mind to take in. It had been easier to slip through life, letting it happen around him, not to think or feel.

The bare flat, the empty nights, with his father either working or studying, no Jadda in the kitchen laughing, no smell of cake, no Australian buffet breakfast, just cereal from a cardboard packet, sweet and tasteless stuff that his father had grown used to eating ... or perhaps it was all that they could afford.

The greatest emptiness had been with the man who was his father. Neither had mentioned Jadda, not then, nor in the three years since. Neither spoke

of the past at all, just of what had to be done now —
buying bread, taking the garbage out. Just sometimes
they talked about the future, when his father might
be allowed to be a doctor again, what subjects Faris
might take at school. It was as though a sheet of glass
separated them. They could see each other, but never
really talk.

A school of tired teachers, where it seemed almost
every other student was like him — bewildered — and
too many who could not speak English. No friends.
Too few school computers and even those often didn't
work.

Loneliness that bit deeper than a shark.

Faris walked to school and to the supermarket.
He studied and he watched TV. Thanks to Jadda, he
already knew most of what they studied in his year at
school.

This was Australia. Not the Australia that he had
dreamed of, the Australia he had longed for when he
walked through the door. This was not the Australia
of the golden beach and laughing games.

But it was real. And like Susannah said, real
things can change.

His father passed the medical exams. He was a
doctor again. But he was still a stranger, still tired.
Another move, away from the smelly flat, to a town
even further from the sea.

It was a good house. Not a beautiful one, but Faris
had his own bedroom. Sheep stood like rocks up
on the hill: grey sheep, not like the cloud-like white
ones in Billy's fields. These paddocks were brown, not

green. Faris still had yet to see a kangaroo, except on TV.

A doctor in a country town, it seemed, worked as much of the day and night as a taxi driver in the city. The phone might ring at five am and his father still be absent when Faris poured cereal for breakfast. But this kitchen smelled of food, not cockroaches, because of Mrs Purdon, who came for two hours each afternoon, who cleaned and made stews, which were not the ones he'd known. She made cakes too — not Jadda's cake but ones with fruit or jam and cream.

Doctors made more money than taxi drivers. A new laptop for his birthday. Ten-dollar notes slipped into Faris's hand so he could buy chocolates after school, and remember David, and the way Susannah carefully nibbled the filling from her chocolate on the beach.

School was different here: older, colder buildings, but students laughed here. To his surprise Faris found that he was doing well.

There were only four boys in his advanced maths class: Joel, who flushed whenever a girl came near; Alex from Belarus, who collected facts and recycled jokes from the previous night's TV shows, which was annoying; Walter, whose family owned most of the grey sheep and who knew everything about aviation, from how far a helicopter could fly to how to land a Harrier jet on a computer simulation, and who liked to order them around, though he just grinned when anyone objected. Faris thought Billy would have got on well with Walter. Or maybe not. Maybe they were too alike.

There was a place outside the library where the four of them sat at lunchtime, to talk about computers and new games, to eat their lunch then go into the library to see if they could land a Harrier jet too. When at mid-year they started to hang their lunchboxes on the tree outside the library — too high for anyone else to see — Faris realised that somehow they were friends.

Not friends that you could tell everything to. Walter and Joel could never understand the terror in the night, living so you never turned round when you heard a stranger's tears, how you readied yourself to always drop at the sound of gunfire.

Perhaps Alex knew. But neither he nor Faris spoke of what they had come from, only what the next weeks or years might bring.

Even Alex, he thought, would not understand a refuge that wasn't really there. Faris knew he was already different enough from the other students without being thought crazy.

He looked at the young man in the too-short school uniform in the mirror.

Was he crazy?

Back in the smelly flat, when Faris woke one night screaming after a nightmare about a wave, his father had explained 'post-traumatic stress disorder', told him how your body got used to being scared and imagined other terrors to explain the chemicals inside you that kept the terror there.

Had the fear chemicals of his body created the illusion that he had once known a small golden beach? Had he imagined the friendships there as well?

If only he could talk to them now, or even text or email them. Would he ever find friendship with that depth again?

Even now, after three years, he longed for his friends so deeply that he could shut his eyes and almost feel that they were there. Billy, shouting with laughter; Juhi, running bare-legged up the beach; Susannah, watching and caring for them all.

Did that mean he had imagined them?

He had tried, many times, to find some clue that they might have actually existed, to discover what had happened to them. He'd Googled their names, hunted for telephone numbers. But there were thousands of Higgses, and Murphys too. He didn't even know the others' surnames, nor had he been able to find any mention of a girl from Sri Lanka called Nafeesa. Only Susannah knew all the names, knew where each was from — if she had even been real herself.

Perhaps Nafeesa was far in the future. Perhaps she and the others were made from his mind's chemicals and would never be there to find.

Faris looked at the boy in the mirror wearing the school uniform. Today he would eat cereal for breakfast, go to school and laugh at lunchtime with his friends.

This was real life. And it was good. Not wonderful. But good.

Mrs Purdon was polishing the bookcases when he came back from school. Mrs Purdon loved polishing. She cleaned the floors like it was a duty, did the washing too, but any spare minute during the two hours a day that Faris's father paid her for was spent polishing. There wasn't much wood in the house, but what there was gleamed.

'Good day at school?'

'Yes.' He didn't tell her that he had topped the class in chemistry. Mrs Purdon's niece was in his class. Faris suspected Mrs Purdon resented, just a bit, this stranger coming to her town and doing better than her family.

'That's good. Letter for you on the table,' said Mrs Purdon, as she turned her back, still carefully polishing, obviously intensely curious.

'For me?' He had never received a letter before. Official letters were sent to his father, not to him. No one from his past life before the refugee camp would dare to write to him, in case it put them in danger too.

He picked up the letter, looked at the name on the envelope and frowned. *The Sisters of St Joseph*. He opened it.

Mrs Purdon looked at him, polishing cloth in her hand. 'Who's it from?'

'A woman who says she's my sister Margaret-Mary.' He shook his head. 'But I don't have a sister.'

Mrs Purdon took the letter. She read the single paragraph quickly. 'She's a nun, love. Nuns are called "Sister". You wouldn't have them, would you, not where you come from? The St Joey's Sisters used to run a school here, years ago.'

She smiled at the memory. 'That's the school I went to, and my mum and dad too. The state school

216

wasn't here then, just this little two-roomed place. Sister Therese and Sister Mary-Catherine, dressed in these long black habits with white wimples about their faces.' Faris had seen nuns like that in movies. He nodded as she continued. 'Handy with the cane sometimes, but we got the best education in Australia from those nuns, I reckon.'

And so you clean my father's house now, thought Faris.

Mrs Purdon looked at him sharply, almost as though he had said the words. 'I reckon half the government was taught by the St Joey's nuns. They took kids who'd never had a chance, got them scholarships to university.' She looked down at the letter. 'This Sister Margaret-Mary wants you to go see her in Sydney. Have you met her somewhere?'

'I've never met a nun.' The faces from his first year in Australia had blurred together, but he was sure none had been dressed in black robes with white wimples.

Mrs Purdon smiled at him. 'You mightn't know you had. They wear clothes like anyone else now, with just a cross around their necks, or a special pin or ring. They do a lot of work with refugees. She probably wants to know how you're getting on.'

It was possible. He thought of the many women he had met, women across desks, the women who had appeared with a big pot of soup and pastries the day after he had arrived at his father's tiny flat, the school uniform they'd brought him too — second-hand, which made him cringe, but better than no uniform at all.

There were many women he had forgotten, because his mind had been too full.

He supposed that she was one of those.

'Well, will you go?'

He had no wish to meet again any of those whose lives he had passed through in his first year in Australia. His mind had carefully kept the world a blur, because if he looked too close the loss of Jadda, his friends and the beach would be too hard to bear.

But he would like an excuse to go back to Sydney. Not the Sydney of the smelly flat, but to try to find the Sydney he had seen on the internet so many years before, the harbour and a thousand small white sails, tourists smiling from the stairs of the Opera House, holding dripping ice-creams in their hands.

Maybe he and Joel and the others could take the train up together, and stay at a hotel.

'I might,' he said.

'Can I go, Dad?' The word 'Dad' had once felt strange. But it had seemed right to give this new father a new name, the name that an Australian boy would call his father.

His father looked at the letter again. 'If you like. I could take a weekend off. A holiday.' He said it in the tone of a man who hadn't taken such a thing for ten years, had perhaps forgotten exactly what it was, but knew that it existed.

Faris stared. It had never occurred to him that his father would have the time to go to Sydney, would even want to. Being with his father would mean awkward silences, instead of laughter with his friends. But he couldn't bring himself to say, 'I don't want you to come.'

'It would be good to meet those who speak my own tongue again,' said his father.

Faris looked at his father in surprise. Faris even thought in English these days. It hadn't occurred to him that his father might miss the language he had grown up with, want to see people from his own land. His father hesitated. 'We could go to the zoo.'

'I'd rather go to the Apple Store,' said Faris. He had read about it: all glass and gadgets. You could see anything online, of course, but there it would be real.

'The Apple Store then. And perhaps a concert.' His father looked at Faris almost warily as he added, 'I have always wanted to hear a concert in the Opera House.'

Would the music at a real concert have the magic of David's playing? For a moment his mind slipped back to the magic world of beach and laughter.

'It will be fun,' his father said, bringing Faris to the present. The word 'fun' was said tentatively, as though it was as odd to him as 'holiday'.

OK, thought Faris. Apple Store. Opera House. Worth a trip to Sydney even if it came with his father's company and a meeting with a strange woman whose life had once touched his, so she thought she knew him. 'Can we go to Bondi Beach too?'

'Of course! We can swim in the baths ...'

'No,' said Faris quickly. He had managed to swim in the school pool. Just. The school pool smelled of

chlorine, not of salt and fear. His body still rebelled at
the thought of touching the sea. 'I'd just like to see an
Australian beach.'

Small waves and blue sky, he thought, and hot
sand on my feet.

CHAPTER 30

Sydney, Australia

The rain gusted across the beach. Out on the grey waves two surfboarders in black wetsuits twisted and balanced, like human performing seals.

It should have been depressing — grey sky again, grey sea. Instead Faris felt strangely content. Real life, he thought. Tomorrow the sky might be blue again. The grey was temporary, no longer a stain across his life.

'Lunch?' suggested his father. He wore a new shirt with his grey work trousers.

Faris nodded.

The restaurant perched above the beach. They sat cautiously, facing each other. Faris wondered if the waiter and the other customers could tell that he had never sat at a table with a thick napkin and heavy cutlery like this. He glanced at his father and realised he was also uncertain. But there was a hint of defiance too, as though this man wished to declare that once he had eaten often in expensive places like this, and now he would again.

His father picked up the menu. 'Flathead tails in beer batter with tartare sauce, matchstick potatoes?'

'Stuck-up chish and fips,' said Faris automatically. It was what he'd have said to Joel and the others. He looked up to find his father grinning.

He couldn't remember his father grinning before.

The bread rolls were good. Faris had forgotten how bread could taste, after the sliced packaged stuff he had eaten for three years in Australia. The fish was wonderful, the chips nothing like the frozen ones Mrs Purdon heated.

The waiter placed a salad bowl on the table. Faris bit into lettuce sharp with onions and the sweet crunch of pomegranate seeds.

Jadda had made salad like this. Suddenly he couldn't swallow. He put his knife and fork down politely, pressed his lips together so he wouldn't cry, and stared resolutely out the window.

'Faris?' He felt his father's hand light on his arm. 'I'll pay the bill.'

A minute later his father was back. 'Come on. Let's get out of here.'

They sat on a bench, facing the cloud-swept sea. The tears slid down, cold on his face. Faris hoped no one would notice.

He had yet to speak Jadda's name to this man, his father and Jadda's son. In three years nothing important had passed between them. Their life was only now, not then.

The silence stretched. The waves danced grey lace across the sand.

'It's my fault.' The words from the man beside him

seemed cracked, as though they had to break to get out of him. 'Everything that has happened to you, to Jadda. All my fault.'

'No.'

'Yes. It has been.'

And it was. Of course it was. If his father had acted differently, they might all be as they had been, with no thought of ever coming to Australia. Without the years of fear, the journey and the shipwreck, Jadda might not have had a stroke, or had a smaller one that she could have survived.

The wind gusted from the sea. It smelled of sunscreen and frying chips. It smelled of memory and the sea. The sheet of glass between him and his father shattered.

Suddenly he heard Susannah's voice. *We can only do what we think is right.*

'Do you think you did what was right? Stopping to help that man?'

'Yes.' The word came with no hesitation. 'The only thing I did wrong was not staying with him, trying to get the police to take him to hospital, even if they took him to prison later. I am a doctor. A doctor's duty is to help. Even when I was a taxi driver, I was a doctor.'

Faris shrugged. 'Well then.'

'You mean that you forgive me?'

Faris watched the waves. No, he thought, I don't forgive you. You did a doctor's duty to a bleeding rebel. You failed in a father's duty to your son, a son's duty to his mother.

Which was more important? He didn't know.

'I miss Jadda,' he said instead. Stupid words. Inadequate. But suddenly he heard a sob from the man beside him.

'I wish I had been there. I wish I could have said ...' His father's voice broke off. And then he said, 'She was so strong. It was embarrassing, when I was growing up, having a mother who spoke out as Jadda did. I worried that someone at her school would report her. "Do what is right," she said, "and bear on your shoulders what comes next. Don't let them make you less than you are."'

Faris looked at his father, wondering. It had never occurred to him that Jadda had helped create his father, the man who risked his family to help a stranger. Perhaps, he thought suddenly, Jadda's outspokenness made the police believe her son might be a rebel.

'What would you have said to her?'

The man beside him shrugged. 'That I loved her, I suppose.'

Faris thought back to those years of phone calls, the expression on Jadda's face as she listened to her son, his distant voice across the world. 'She knew,' he said.

'I thank you.' His father's words were formal. But he smiled at his son.

The rain gusted again, then stopped. They caught a bus — Faris realised his father avoided taxis now — to the city, walked past the Opera House to the Botanic Gardens, where Sister Margaret-Mary had suggested that they meet, and sat in the café while the trees dripped outside. Faris glanced out the windows, trying to judge if any of the women outside looked like a nun.

'Be careful what you tell her,' said his father.

Faris nodded. They had permanent residency, but the safety of Australian citizenship was still to come. Australia treated them well, now, but both knew how quickly that could change. Perhaps he would never speak with the freedom that the other kids at school took for granted, kids who had never known how a few words, a small action, might destroy a life.

Two women entered. One was middle-aged, a bit like Mrs Purdon. The other was so old she had shrunk, but her eyes as they looked around the café were clear green. She saw him. She said something to her companion. The companion nodded and left the café as the old woman made her way alone through the chairs.

Faris and his father stood politely.

'Well, boyo,' said the old woman, a small cross sitting on her pale green cardigan, smiling through her wrinkles with those familiar green eyes.

All at once he understood.

CHAPTER 31

He stood in shock, cold and hot all at the same time.

Susannah held out her hand: freckled, shaking slightly, but the small hand he remembered nonetheless.

'You must be Faris's father.' Her voice was forthright and direct, the voice of a woman who was used to students obeying. 'I'm Sister Margaret-Mary. Faris and I met three years ago. Would you mind if we talked alone?'

'Is it about the application for citizenship?'

'No. I'm nothing official. We met, that's all. I would like to talk to him now.'

Faris tried to find his breath. 'I'll be fine, Dad. We're ... friends. I just didn't recognise the name.'

'Friends?' Faris could see his father's puzzlement as he looked from the ancient woman to his son, could see the moment he accepted that his son was in so many ways still a stranger; he could see the flash of pain this caused too.

For the first time Faris realised how much his dad wanted to be his true father. He understood the barriers that had held back the words of love, could even glimpse a future where the trust between them might grow. He gave his father a quick hug, startling them both. 'Go and look at the Opera House,' he suggested.

His father looked from Faris to Susannah. 'I'll come back ... in an hour then?'

'An hour would be fine.' Susannah's accent was still there, faint: the song of Ireland. 'Tea,' she said to Faris. 'Hot and sweet. That's what we need.'

He nodded.

He had drunk half the cup before he felt he could speak. Susannah was always good at giving you time for silence, he thought. Days or weeks, to let your mind catch up. He had longed for his friends. He had never realised how much time would have ripped them away from him.

Sitting with Susannah now he almost felt more lonely than he had been before he met her again.

'You became a nun.' And old, he thought. So old.

She smiled. 'What else should I be, after eighty years of caring for you all?'

Faris had looked up the Sisters of St Joseph on Google before he and his father had come to Sydney. He had wondered why any woman would join a religious order and give up a family and love.

The ten-year-old girl had given up her own life for the children on the beach. But that girl had been rich in both love and family. He looked at Susannah's face. He suspected this old woman was as rich as the girl had been.

'Why aren't you called Susannah? I thought nuns could use their own names now.'

'Susannah is my middle name. I thought Margaret-Mary boring. I thought, in Australia I'll be Susannah. A new land and a new name. But when I got here,' she sipped her tea, 'I found that I was still Margaret-Mary.'

Yes, she was still his friend. Impossible, that a woman so old — more than grandmother old — might be a friend. 'You're Susannah too.'

'Well, I suppose I am at that. I'm so very sorry it took so long to find you. I hoped I could be there when you first arrived.'

She looked at Faris steadily. 'It's always hard when you get here. Even for those who come here knowing they will be allowed to stay. At least I knew Australia wanted me, that Australians spoke my language. It was bad for Jamila and the others who left Refuge just before you came. But you never told me your last name. Just that your father was a doctor. I wish you could have had someone who could say, "Those days on the beach happened."'

'Yes.' He wasn't sure what he felt now. Relief — his mind wasn't so damaged that he had imagined it all. A sense of wonder. Happiness too, because he *had* survived. He had even begun to grasp life again and make it good.

'Did you think you might have imagined it all too?' he asked.

Susannah sipped her tea. 'Of course. Nikko wasn't with me when I woke up, you see. I'd been delirious. The beach was just a fever dream, I told myself. But I had changed. Even Mam knew that I had changed. You can't do what we did back there and return just the same. I met David and knew it had been real. It was twenty-six years later. You know how time hiccupped back on Refuge.'

Refuge. A good name for it, he thought. His heart had suddenly worked out how to beat again.

Susannah shook her head at the memory. 'There was David, in my schoolyard. A bit more meat on his bones and his poor scarred hands. A Jewish boy in a Catholic school in a little country town, but his aunt knew our children got the best that we could give them. That's what mattered. Oh, those were hard years. Half the children didn't speak English and had ghosts in their eyes.'

He stared at her in wonder. So the friends from his bright golden beach were here — or two of them at least. But he still felt the ache of loss. They would be too old to want to play with a ball on the beach. 'Did David recognise you?'

'We wore habits back then, long robes and veils, all black and white. I doubt he even looked at my face at first. I called him up to the office. "Where is your violin, David?" I asked him. "Gone," he said. And then he said, "Susannah," and we were both crying, and I had to explain why to Sister Augustine. Nothing fazed Sister Augustine, not even the tiger snake under the blackboard.'

'Did Sister Augustine believe you?'

'She found David a violin. She found him a music teacher, when his aunt married and they went to live in Melbourne. His teacher had played with the Berlin Symphony Orchestra before they put him in the concentration camp, and now his hands were as bad as David's. Oh, they were good for each other, those two. They helped each other build new lives.'

She hadn't answered his question about Sister Augustine. Somehow he knew that she never would answer him, not about the women she called sisters.

'Where is David now?' He glanced around the café, in case one of the men might suddenly turn out to be the boy he'd known.

'He died,' said Susannah — Sister Margaret-Mary — gently. 'A few years ago. He had a good long life, Faris. A rich one.'

He knew she didn't mean in money.

'He became a psychiatrist, helping those with mental illnesses. He knew enough about grief and loss, didn't he now. He knew how to help. He played with a string quartet. Not to big audiences, but he was happy with it. Played at one of my schools a few times. I taught in every little town in Victoria at some stage, I think. Little school after little school.

'I started looking for you all, after David. Not by myself, of course, but I'd ask the brother-in-law of a pupil's mother, or a girl I'd once taught, anyone who might know about new immigrants. Sister Augustine and I were on the wharf when Nikko's boat arrived from Greece. No, I don't know why he wasn't with me. Perhaps in his heart he wanted his true family.' She grinned. It was a clear echo of the ten-year-old's grin. 'No one thinks to ask a nun why she's there when she might be needed, and we were needed indeed. It got me into the detention centre to meet Jamila too.'

'She's safe? Happy?' How many of them might be still alive? He tried to work out their ages. His mind had always baulked at trying it before, in case it had been an illusion and he was adding to it. 'What about Nikko?'

'A crewman leaped down into the sea to rescue him. Oh, Nikko grew so tall, taller even than you are now.' She chuckled. 'Though not quite as tall as those uncles he imagined at that Feast of St Kangarou. Nikko became a teacher. He married another teacher — the crewman's niece — years later. They're retired, but he and his wife stay with isolated children around Australia to help them with correspondence school. Ah, it came good. With a bit of faith and a lot of tears and work.

'Jamila has one of those computer jobs.' She spoke in the tones of one who regarded computers as items from a strange world, far more foreign than the lands they all had come from. 'She has a PhD, the girl who couldn't go to school. It hasn't been easy for her. But she's going to stand for parliament in the next election. She says she'll be prime minister one day.'

'Is she married?'

'Not yet. But I think she will be, one day.'

Faris wondered how Jamila's dreams for Australia had changed from the city of women she had imagined as a terrified child on a drifting boat. Susannah nodded, as if she knew what he was thinking. 'She has a vision for Australia's future too.'

'How did she survive?'

'She and her parents fought the man who tried to kill them. Jamila tied him up with her scarf. Her father paid the crew and other passengers not to untie him. Jamila says she and her parents explained what the man had done to the officials here, but she doesn't know what happened to him.'

In a funny way it hurt, thinking his friends had led their lives without him. All of them so much older than him now.

'Are they OK?' He was really asking if they had been injured, even mutilated, by whatever horror they had gone back to.

Again Susannah understood without the words. 'We each have scars, of some sort or other. The fever left me deaf in one ear. Who needs two, when one will do?' She put her hand on his; it was small, cold and old, but comforting. 'I think that each one of us is happy. Maybe we learned *how* to be happy, back on that beach. We meet every year, just after Christmas. You can see for yourself.'

'What about Billy? Did you ever find out what happened to him? I tried to Google him, but there are so many Higgses.'

Susannah laughed, delighted. 'You'll never guess. I taught his great-grandchildren! Billy had the biggest farm in the district and fourteen children. He married his cook. And oh, Faris, you will like this. One great-great-grandson became an astronaut! A scientist, up in space.'

Faris thought of Billy's journey in the stinking hold of the small sailing ship. Billy would have understood his great-great-grandson's journey and been proud.

'We've tracked down nearly all of us, even the ones I knew before you joined us. Even Ah Goon. He got back to China. He wrote a poem that is still taught today, about a far bright beach. There's a bay named after Henri — he got here too, and then back to France. Pedro's many-times-great-grandson has written a story about his seafaring ancestor, who went to Australia and back. Mei Ling died in a car crash, the day before her fiftieth birthday. But she left two daughters — oh, such fine girls. She became a pianist, a composer of music for movies. All those concerts of David's perhaps. Bridget was a nurse in World War One, Julio became mayor of Bellagong. Did I ever tell you about Julio? I'll tell you about them all one day. Too much to tell you now.'

Yes. It was all too much.

'What about Mudurra and Juhi?'

'They are too far back for history. But I think they are with us nonetheless. Have you ever wondered who was the first person to step onto Australia? Maybe it was Mudurra.'

'With Juhi beside him?'

She laughed again. It was the girl's laugh, from the old woman. 'Why not? Maybe he dreamed Australia just like he dreamed the beach. Maybe without him none of us would be here.'

'But Juhi hasn't changed the world. There's still hatred. People still kill each other because of their religion or the colour of their skin. She hasn't changed a thing.'

Susannah met his gaze. 'Who knows? Give us time, boyo. The world keeps changing. Maybe in time there'll be no hatred. But I think that she and Mudurra were happy. Don't you?'

Faris thought of Juhi's face as she followed Mudurra through the doorway — the modern girl who had been the best student in her school. 'I don't know. If only she could have taken some things with her. Like antibiotics, in case she got sick. But we couldn't take anything, could we? Not even your book.'

Her face was serene. 'We took our memories. We took something else as well.'

'What?'

'The gift of friendship. Every one of us, bruised and battered by other people. We learned understanding there. We learned that together we were strong.'

Faris thought of Alex, Walter and Joel. Was his friendship with them a gift from Refuge too? He remembered one of Alex's stupid facts, that Indigenous people had plants that were sometimes more effective medicines than modern drugs. Had Juhi also known that?

There was a name he had avoided. He spoke it now. 'Nafeesa?'

As soon as he said it, he knew this was who mattered most. It wasn't just that Nafeesa might be closest to his own time and close to him in age. He had felt a string bind them together from the first moment he had seen the love and determination in her eyes, so like Jadda's.

Once more he felt the warmth of Nafeesa's fingers touching his.

'Ah, yes. Nafeesa.' Susannah looked at Faris steadily. 'I worked out all the times in my book, you know. When each of us had come from, the date we'd go back to. But I didn't get a chance to ask Nafeesa when she'd come from, not before the doorway was washing away.'

'Nafeesa arrived after me. That means she'll arrive in Australia after me too.' But would that be years, or months later? he wondered. He simply didn't know.

Did Susannah?

'You want to meet her when she gets here?'

'Of course! I want to meet everyone,' he added quickly.

'But her especially?'

Faris was silent. This was an old woman, after all. How could she understand?

'We were all equal on that beach,' said Susannah, her voice clear even among the mutter and chatter of the café. 'The colour of our skin didn't matter, nor how we prayed to God, or where we came from. But it matters here in Australia. Are you sure you'll want Nafeesa for a friend now? A girl from a culture so different from yours?'

'I would still be her friend.' He thought of Nafeesa's determination, holding the doorway on the beach. 'She wouldn't let differences stop her from being my friend either. Not Nafeesa.'

'Even if her uncle didn't approve? Your father?'

Faris thought of the man in tears on the bench by the sea. 'My father is a good man. I think he is a man who accepts others as they are.'

'And his son is too?'

Faris put up his chin. 'Yes.'

235

Susannah drained her teacup. 'I thought so, boyo. I knew you well, back there. But people change.'

Faris looked at her, a challenge in his eyes. 'I'm going to look for Nafeesa too. If we all made it to Australia, then she will as well. I'll be there to help her. I ... I've got some money saved. I can buy her a phone, so we can text, even if she's in another city. If she doesn't arrive till I'm older and I've got a job, then I can help her even more. And if she doesn't come for ten years, twenty years, when you are gone, I'll still be there for her —'

Susannah held up an age-spotted hand. 'Enough. I believe you.' She looked out the window.

Faris wondered if she was looking for the companion who had brought her here. Was she tired? Did she need to rest?

He said quickly, in case the companion arrived, 'Why did it happen? How could it happen? The more I think about it, the less I understand.'

'I've had over eighty years to think about it,' said Sister Margaret-Mary, looking back at him. 'And I don't understand it either. But I no longer think we need to understand everything in life. It happened. It was good.'

'Because it taught us friendship?'

She smiled. 'It gave us time. Time to want to live. But we learned more than that. It taught us how to live together, despite our differences, how to work together too.'

'You think that's why we all survived when we came back?'

236

'We each had such a strong vision of what Australia should be when we arrived at Refuge. Refuge let us share each other's visions.' She met his eyes. 'I think, no, I believe, that each one of us who was at Refuge has made a difference in this world. Will make a difference too. Every one of us.'

'Even me?'

'Don't get too swollen-headed, boyo.' Somehow the strong lilt of her childhood was back. 'But yes ... you too.'

'I was so scared. I thought maybe I was mad.' His voice broke. And he was crying, sobbing fully as he had never been able to sob in the last three years. Sobbing for the loss of Jadda, for the loss of the childhood he'd never had. Crying because he was happy too for the life that might be to come.

Susannah put her arm around him, just as she had so many times for all of them, back at the beach. The other patrons looked away, embarrassed.

At last the tears stopped. 'I'm sorry.'

'Don't be.'

'I ... I don't know why I am crying now.'

'Because it's over,' she said quietly. 'And it's beginning. You know what we all do when we meet each year? We go down to the beach. Not just the friends you met at Refuge, but some of the ones who left before you as well: Jane, Vlad, Julio, Abdulla. We play the game too.'

He tried to think of a nun in black robes playing the game, or the old woman in front of him. 'Even you?'

'Even me,' Susannah said. 'Even David in that last year in his wheelchair, and the children and grandchildren too. And I'll tell you something, boyo, every child on the beach joins in. No matter what their faith or colour. Refuge is still there, Faris, as long as love and memory live. Day by day, we change the world.'

Suddenly the scent of tea bags and reheated cakes vanished. He could smell Jadda's hand cream, feel her warmth. All those days or weeks or years on the beach and she'd been there, and by the same power she was with him still.

She always would be, as long as love and memory remained. Jadda helped make me who I am, he thought. If I help change the world, Jadda's hands will be there too.

He looked at the old woman next to him, fragile, fulfilled. Saw the old woman and the girl.

'I am more than ninety years old,' she said softly. 'But I think I can toss a ball on a beach for a few years yet. I hope you will be with us too.'

'I will,' he said. He leaned over and kissed Susannah's cheek.

CHAPTER 32

His father arrived as Susannah started on a second cup of tea and a slice of banana cake. She didn't look tired. Almost, thought Faris, as if she is waiting for something to happen.

His father looked almost warily from his son to the old woman forking in cake. 'Everything OK?'

'Yes. All OK. Thanks, Dad.'

'Sit down,' invited Susannah. 'The banana cake is good.' She turned to Faris. 'Off you go for a walk. Your father and I can have a talk.'

Suddenly it was as though they were back at Refuge, with Susannah plotting — always for their own good, but plotting still — up on her sand hill.

Faris looked at her suspiciously. 'What do you want to talk to him about?'

'Faris!' said his father, obviously surprised by his son's lack of manners with an old woman.

Susannah laughed. 'Oh, your son knows me well. Off you go, boyo. I want to convince your father to spend next Christmas at a beach, where you can play a game on the sand. Does that satisfy you?'

It didn't. But Faris knew that was all he was going to get. Susannah might have spent a long life being

Sister Margaret-Mary, but she'd spent eighty years being Susannah too.

What was she planning now?

'Take the path down to the harbour,' said Susannah. 'Just a quick breath of fresh air, there and back. There's a lovely apartment you can both stay in at the beach,' she added to his father. 'It's in a block of units that belongs to an old friend of mine, Nikkodemus Simoneides. Faris has met him. You can help us celebrate the Feast of St Kangarou too.' Her smile had a touch of wickedness.

'I'm not sure —' began his father.

Faris grinned. 'Don't worry, Dad. St Kangarou isn't part of a religion.' He stood up. 'I won't be long.'

His father sat next to Susannah, obviously puzzled, and just as obviously waiting till his son would choose to tell him what was happening here, how he came to know a nun so well she'd want him to visit at Christmas, how he knew a man who owned holiday apartments by the sea, and why he should celebrate a Feast of St Kangarou.

Faris realised that his father had also waited patiently for his son to talk about Jadda, about all the things that had hurt too much to speak of.

Until today. Suddenly he knew he liked this man. He'd had to love him. There had been no one else in the last three years to love. But Faris was proud his father was a man who he liked now.

Tonight I will tell him how strong Jadda was on the boat, thought Faris. Tell him that Jadda spoke of him, just before she died. How much she loved us both. All of life is a voyage, he thought. My father and I are still sailing. But finally he could feel the joy and wonder of the journey.

One day, maybe, he might even tell his father about the beach, about Refuge. Even if he didn't believe in its reality, this man would understand. And when Faris was ready, he would reach back, into that day of grief and terror, and see the wave as beautiful, majestic, as it reached towards the sky. There was no hatred in a wave. It simply was.

'See you in twenty minutes,' he said.

Susannah smiled. 'There's all the time you need. Banana cake,' she added to his father, 'and coffee, I'm guessing, not tea? You look like a coffee man to me.'

Faris walked down between the trees. The harbour waves slapped at the sea wall. No beach, no breakfast buffets, no kangaroos grazing under orange trees in suburban streets, no pet koalas who sat on your lap and ate chicken, nothing at all of the Australia he'd dreamed up. But Faris was the happiest he had ever been.

We'll play the game on the beach again, he thought. My father too. Perhaps he'll learn to laugh more.

Suddenly he wondered what Dad would think of Jamila. She would be closer to his father's age than his. He grinned at the idea of Jamila as a stepmother, or his father as husband to a prime minister. Impossible ...

But then the impossible had happened. He shook his head, still smiling, and turned to go back. Would the concert tonight be as good as David's playing?

241

Perhaps he'd cry, in the dimness of the audience. It felt good to be able to cry at last.

Three girls walked along the path next to the harbour wall, licking ice-creams. The younger girls wore jeans and T-shirts. The tallest wore a long blue top, embroidered and edged with gold, over plain white trousers. Her long black hair was drawn back in a single plait, the sides held with two gold-coloured combs. A silky scarf was draped across her hair and neck, in gold and blue.

She pointed the way to the café, then said something to the younger girls, obviously intending to head up that way.

She was too young. No, Faris thought, it is I who am older. Three years older than when I left Refuge. Older by a year or two, perhaps, than she is now.

Something he had never felt before washed through him. Susannah had planned this. Known about them both. Plotted their meeting. Perhaps had planned that they wouldn't meet, if all Faris had been through had made him angry and intolerant.

But he had passed her test.

This girl was a stranger, with a different past, from a different culture. Even here, he realised, in the real world, each person had his or her own Australia. But people could still share dreams, forging a world they knew was good. And this stranger had shared more with him than any other girl he'd ever meet.

The girl saw him. Her face broke into a smile of joy. 'Faris!'

Suddenly Faris could smell orange blossom, feel the hot golden sand, see the years stretch before him, each one richer than the last.

'Nafeesa,' he whispered.

The little girls stared as Faris ran towards their sister.

AUTHOR'S NOTES

My various ancestors all came here by boat, of one sort or another, from many places, at many different times. All of them were fleeing persecution or hardship, or dreaming of a better life.

People have sailed across the dangerous ocean to Australia for perhaps the last sixty thousand years. Probably they always will, as long as there are humans and boats to sail in.

This book explores the stories of some of those who have made that voyage. It is never easy to leave your land and your people.

I don't believe that any nation — including Australia — has a duty to accept everyone who wants to live there, or who arrives on its shores. This is a world where there can be three million refugees a year, or far more. There are many millions more who would like to leave a poor nation and live in a rich one. No country can ever say these days, 'Let them all come,' without destroying its land and social structures. I am glad that I don't have to make the decisions about who and how many should live here, although I think that all Australians should be part of that debate.

But we also have a duty to try to understand the grief and tragedies of others, and to accept that, as an island nation, strangers always have and always will — somehow — arrive here by sea.

In *Pennies for Hitler* I wrote that hatred is contagious, but so is kindness. Sometimes being good to others — as a nation, or as individuals — can be as powerful as guns.

My grandmother was proud that she greeted visitors with a cup of tea, and fresh scones or apple tea cake. No matter who the new arrivals are, or what they have done — or for how long we decide they should stay — we owe them the equivalent of Grandma's welcome: a cup of tea, a scone (and the best education and medical help while they are here) and compassion.

Yes, we should plan and examine carefully who and how many people come to Australia and in what way. But we should always remember that our families were in those boats too.

Faris's homeland

I have deliberately kept the details of Faris's homeland vague. Faris could be from one of many countries where, if you speak out against the government, or are of a race or religion that isn't that of the ruling party, you might be tortured and imprisoned, and your family too. For the same reason I have not mentioned his religion, skin colour, or the year this story is set. The boy on the cover of this book is the designer's image of Faris — a good one, but perhaps not mine or yours.

Immigration laws, regulations and practices

The immigration requirements mentioned in this book may differ from the ones in place by the time you read it. Australia's immigration laws, regulations and practices constantly change as circumstances do.

The Faris in this book arrived in Australia as a thirteen-year-old boy who had accurate and detailed papers with him, proving both his identity and his history. He also had a father who would already have been assessed as not being a security risk, and who already had residence in Australia, with good prospects of being accepted for citizenship. At the time I wrote this book it appeared that in a case like Faris's the case workers assigned to him would probably have arranged for him to fairly swiftly join his father. This, however, is supposition. The government agencies contacted stated that much would depend 'on circumstances', without specifying what those circumstances might be, nor did websites give a definitive answer. I had the impression — which may not be accurate — that case workers might be allowed leeway in assessing what might happen, depending on the boy's circumstances.

These notes would be a good place to discuss Australia's immigration practices, but as I write this, the laws and regulations are undergoing considerable change, with a great deal of discussion and many differing points of view. It is likely that the next two years, at least, will see even more changes. Anything I write now would probably be out of date even before this book is printed.

St Kangarou

There is, of course, no St Kangarou. Many thanks to Liz Kemp, for suggesting that St Kangaroo should end in the Greek 'ou' (and for her insistence on making the original story richer too).

Susannah

Susannah — Sister Margaret-Mary — and Sister Augustine are not based on any real person, especially not any of the members of the Sisters of St Joseph. But in my childhood I saw those indomitable women fight for the best possible education for barefoot kids. Back in the days when many schools found some pretext to exclude Indigenous kids, and when girls weren't supposed to beat boys in debating, the Sisters made an Indigenous girl captain of their debating team.

The team won the championship. I still wonder how it changed those girls' lives too. Perhaps their lives also changed Australia. This book is for those women, with honour and gratitude.

The game

About a decade ago, on a South Australian beach, I watched a game that went on for all the days I was there. People joined it, people left, young, old, different clothes or different-coloured skins. It was the simplest game I've ever seen, and perhaps the richest too.

David's music

As a child, the man who taught me the violin had David's hands and history. He was a good man, generous, and I think happy, despite all that he had lost.

Susannah's list

1. *Mudurra* — fourteen years old at Refuge. Born in what is now East Timor circa 60,000 BCE. Arrived in a canoe, fleeing a volcanic eruption. Married Juhi.

2. *Ah Goon* — thirteen years old at Refuge. Born in Peking (modern-day Beijing). He was part of an exploration fleet ordered by Emperor Yung-Lo, commanded by the Grand Eunuch Zheng He, which sailed in 1421. Ah Goon was washed overboard in a storm circa 1422. Married (?). Had at least one child, a son, when he returned to China. High-ranking public servant and author of the poem 'The Golden Beach' (see translation by Mei Ling McDonald).

3. *Pedro (surname uncertain)* — twelve years old at Refuge. Born in Portugal. He was ill from scurvy when he arrived in 1522 on a ship commanded by his uncle Cristóvão de Mendonça in a search for the 'Isles of Gold' (*Ilhas do Ouro*) beyond Sumatra. A Pedro de Mendonça captained the *Ilhas do Ouro* in 1544.

4. *Jan van Klomp* — ten-year-old son of an important man (supercargo — the person who supervises the cargo) on the Dutch ship *Arnhem* in 1623. Suffered from scurvy. Cape Arnhem and Arnhem Land in Australia are named after Jan's ship, which itself was named after the Netherlands city of Arnhem. Jan survived scurvy, and later shipwreck. It is probable he is the Jan van Klomp who later became a famous astronomer. Twice married; eight children; died in 1708.

5. Henri Bouvier — twelve years old at Refuge. Born in Marseilles, France, in 1760. He arrived on the *Gros Ventre* as part of the expedition of Louis François de Saint Allouarn, who claimed the west coast of Australia for France in 1772. Unable to determine what part of the coast Henri came ashore; he only knew they had been sailing along it for 'some days'. Henri was suffering from scurvy, but recovered with the fresh food in Australia. An Henri Bouvier is listed as a captain in Napoleon's army circa 1800; probably the same Henri Bouvier who became a wine merchant and grape grower in 1801. Chateau Bouvier is still owned by the family and the 'De Or' label is well known, with wine cellars open to the public; see Nikko's letter, 1982. Seventeen children; wife Margrete.

6. Billy (William) Higgs — fifteen years old at Refuge. Born in London, England, in 1814. Arrived in Australia as a convict in 1829. Married Mary Higginbotham in 1845 and had fourteen children, including William, Susannah, Bridget, Mary and Nicholas; see chart from Higgs family tree. Died in 1902. Great-great-grandson Arthur (Artie) Harrison engineer and astronaut.

7. John Grady (Big Johnny) — thirteen years old at Refuge. Born in Manchester, England, in 1822. Press-ganged into the crew of the ship *Mary Castle* in 1834 and shipwrecked in 1835. Arrived at Refuge after the shipwreck. Rescued and arrived in Cape Town in 1835. He arrived in Hobart in 1836 as a crewmember on the *Anglesea*. He jumped ship — the *Anglesea* — in Hobart in 1836; was granted land in the Midlands of Van Diemen's Land (modern Tasmania) in 1841. Married Anne Douglass in 1841, no issue; married Jane McDonald in 1843 and had six children: Bill, Henry, Jane, Susan, John and Douglas. John Grady became a magistrate in 1847 and founded Grady and Henty Agricultural Company in 1848.

8. *Bridget Flaherty* — ten years old at Refuge. Born in Galway, Ireland, in 1839. Reason for leaving — the Irish Potato Famine of 1845–52 and typhoid epidemics. Starved on board ship. Arrived in Australia in 1849. She later wrote to a niece in Ireland that she had survived by making soup from the ship's rats. Present at the Eureka Stockade with her parents in 1852. She married Thomas Burke MP in 1859. They had eight children and she became a prominent reformer for children's health and schooling; said to be the force behind her husband's campaign to end child labour in factories. She was a member of the Women's Suffrage Union. Died in 1919. Great-granddaughter Senator Jessup (contacted). See further notes on the Burke family.

9. *Gow Lee* — born in southern China in Kaiping county, inland from Hong Kong. Arrived in Australia in 1857. Founded *The Worragong Dispatch* in 1867; founded Eagle Publishing in 1872; President of

Worragong Enlistment Committee 1916–18. Married Gladys Green in 1872 and had six children: William, Albert, Susan, John, Henry and Percival. Died in 1939. His son Albert was elected Member for Burrinyup 1923–34. Henry won the Distinguished Conduct Medal; his citation credited him with saving the lives of eight of his comrades. Susan was first female councillor for Worragong and founded *The Gazette*, a literary and political magazine. See Lee family records.

10. *Wolfgang Klaus* — born in Bavaria in 1844. He arrived in Adelaide, Australia, in 1857 and settled on a farm near Mount Pleasant, in the Barossa Valley, in 1862. This is still farmed by his descendants. He married Bertha Smith in 1873 and had seven children: Martha, Heinrich, Wilhelm, Kurt, Annaliese, Susannah and John. See *History of Mount Pleasant* and *Pioneers of the Barossa*.

11. *Miriam Wehby* — born in Lebanon in 1883. Arrived at Refuge in 1890. Landed in Melbourne in 1890. Married a distant relative. Five children. Founded the Henty Department Stores. Died in 1937 of influenza.

12. *Rose Adler* — thirteen years old at Refuge. Born in Bangalore, India, in 1885 (her father was in the English army and her mother was born in Rangoon, Burma). Arrived in Australia in 1898 and married Arthur Bransome in 1902. No children. She was widowed in 1904 and organised the Victorian Women's Nursing Brigade in 1915. She served in Flanders 1915–19;

founded Luton Hills District Hospital in 1922; founded the Estelle Adler Memorial Girls' College in 1924; President of Luton Hills Women's Guild 1932–53 and 1956–83; Director of Commonwealth Education Fund 1952–72; graduated from the University of Melbourne in 1977 and died in 1983.

13 and 14. *Ahmad and Ali (brothers; surname unknown)* — Ahmad was born in 1882 at Makassar in Sulawesi. Ali was born in 1883. Their father, grandfathers and great-grandfathers were trepang collectors and navigators, with enormous knowledge of the Indon archipelago and helped with transport for the sandalwood industry between Timor and northern Australia. Ahmad and Ali arrived in Australia about 1898 and worked in the pearling industry based at Broome. Ahmad was deep underwater when the captain of the ship decided to run for shore as the weather grew suddenly threatening. Ali refused to allow his brother to be brought to the surface too quickly, risking agony and paralysis from 'the bends', and likely death. The brothers stayed on Refuge for only a few hours, working out a strategy for their survival, with little contact with the others. As so little was known about them, it has been difficult to trace their lives in Australia, but they appear to be the two brothers who worked on the *Siren* 1898–99. Ali convinced the captain that they needed Ahmad's knowledge of winds and navigation, taught to him by his father and grandfather, to survive the storm. The two brothers helped bring the ship to Broome safely. Both acted as navigators for pearling ships in the next few years, using their knowledge of both the monsoon winds and currents as well as locating pearling grounds. Their successful boat-building business has been continued by two of their children and three of their grandchildren, its headquarters moving from Broome to Perth. It has recently diversified into underwater exploration for both industrial and scientific expeditions. Ahmad died in a rescue attempt for a stricken ship in 1927. Ali died in 1951, before any of the Refuge survivors could contact him to see if the brothers were indeed those young men who had so briefly paused on the beach.

15. Susannah Murphy (Sister Margaret-Mary) — born in Galway, Ireland, in 1913. Travelled to Australia in 1923. Her illness was never diagnosed: possibly mild polio, but no other cases on board the ship. Suffered mild lower limb paralysis, but within two years this was no longer a problem. Joined the order of the Sisters of St Joseph in 1932.

16. Jane Taylor — twelve years old at Refuge. Born in Surrey, England, in 1930 and arrived at Refuge in 1942. Her family were in Singapore and hoped to evacuate to Australia when Singapore was taken by the Japanese. Instead they were imprisoned from 1942 to 1946. After the war her family decided to return to England. Jane arrived in London, England, in 1946. She became a Lecturer in Political Philosophy at London University in 1955. She didn't come to Australia until 1962, when she was made a Visiting

Fellow at the Australian National University from 1962 to 1965. Jane became Professor of Philosophy, London University, in 1971; Emeritus Professor in 1993 and the editor of *The Journal of International Politics*. From 1966 onwards she has spent Christmas in Australia.

17. *David Weisengarten* — thirteen years old at arrival from Austria in 1945. Graduated from University of Sydney as a doctor in 1959. Married Esther Krantz in 1964 and had three children: Adam, William and Susannah. Founded the Hilde Weisengarten Memorial Music Scholarship; member of the Uncles support group for disadvantaged children; presented with the Order of Australia in 2002. Died in Sydney, Australia, in 2006.

18. *Julio Castelli* — eleven years old at Refuge. He was born in Tuscany, Italy, and left in 1947. He was ill on board ship (measles?) and arrived in Sydney in 1947. Graduated from University of New South Wales in Dentistry in 1965. He married Maria Fitzpatrick in 1977 and they had five children: Sunny, Nicholas, William, Susannah and Emily. He was Mayor of Bellagong for the period 1978–84 and was on the Bellagong Hospital Board from 1970 onwards; founded the Bellagong Junior Soccer Club in 1981; established the Bellagong Scholarship Fund in 1993. Member of the Order of Australia 2004. See Castelli family history.

19. *Nikkodemus Simoneides (Nikko)* — six years old at Refuge. Born in 1946. He was on a ferry to Piraeus in 1952 when he fell from the ferry and was rescued by Simon Petraeus. He arrived in Australia in 1953. He graduated from University of Sydney with a BA in 1965, Dip Ed 1966, MA 1971. He married Maria Petraeus in 1972. See Simoneides family notes for further details.

20. *Mei Ling McDonald* — born in Saigon in 1962. Left Saigon in 1974 and arrived in Darwin, Australia, in 1974. She graduated from the University of Queensland in 1981, having studied Ethnomusicology. She went to the Queensland Conservatorium in 1983 and married Harry McDonald in 1984. She was awarded a Helpmann Award for the score of *Departures* and shortlisted for the Academy Awards for the musical score of the movie *Ride of the Valkyries*. She had two children: Susannah McDonald born in 1987 and Adele McDonald in 1989. She died in a car crash in 2012. See notes by Susannah McDonald.

21. *Rosanna Suttman* — born in Chile in 1968. Arrived at Refuge in 1978. Stayed only two days. B. Law University of Sydney 1992. Worked in the Environmental Defender's Office 1996–98. Senior partner in Suttman, Sparks and Endicott. Amateur ornithologist.

22. *Jamila* — thirteen years old at Refuge. She was born in 1978 in Kabul, Afghanistan. Arrived in Pakistan in 1991, reached Indonesia in 1992 and landed on Christmas Island in 1993. She graduated (Hons, Software Engineering) from Monash University in 1999 and gained her PhD in 2003. She became a contract security consultant for the Department of Foreign Affairs and Trade and founded Data Plus Ltd in 2004. Data Plus was listed on the Australian Stock Exchange in 2007; Jamila retained 51 per cent of shares, but retired from day-to-day management of the company. She founded the White City Scholarship Trust for Girls in 2008. Lives at 'Highview' via Bungendore, NSW. She is campaigning to run as an independent in the federal elections.

23. Vlad Botan (original surname unknown; changed to Lister in Australia) — born in Bosnia in 1982. Arrived at Refuge in 1996. Arrived in Sydney in 1996 and received B. Engineering at the University of Queensland in 2007. Married Melanie Harper (geophysicist) in 2008. Mining engineer, amateur ornithologist, consultant to the Environmental Defender's Office. Presently living and working at Kalgoorlie, WA.

24. Juhi (surname unknown) — born in South Sudan in 1990. Fled Sudan for Ethiopia in 2003. She arrived at Refuge in 2005 and married Mudurra circa 60,000 BCE. May their lives have been blessed forever.

25. Abdulla al-Yussuf — eight years old at Refuge. Stayed less than a day. Circumstances of arrival unknown. Born in southern Iraq in 1999 (town unknown); family fled to Jordan in 2003; arrived at Christmas Island in 2007. High-school student at Armidale, NSW.

ACKNOWLEDGEMENTS

My gratitude to the wonderful Sisters of St Joseph: Sisters Catherine Therese Kane, Mary Harding, Sheila McCreanor, June Madden and Christine Rowan, who entranced me with their stories on a wet afternoon, and shared the histories of the women in their order. The Susannah in this book is not based on any member of the Sisters of St Joseph, but I hope that they feel she would, indeed, have found joining their order inevitable, given her background and eighty years of caring for the children of Refuge.

More thanks than I can express to the ever-wondrous Emeritus Professor Virginia Hooker for her continued suggestions and corrections, providing the names of several of the characters in this book and also their backgrounds. All errors are mine, but her knowledge and extraordinary insights enrich my life and work.

Angela Marshal performed her usual magic, turning a mess of bad spelling into a readable manuscript, and helping the slow evolution of Nafeesa's and Jamila's backgrounds. Her depth of knowledge — and its eclectic breadth — mean that Angela continues to add fresh insights and information for each book.

Fabia Pryor's invaluable research also gave me a wealth of interviews from people who had survived dangers like those in this book. While all the stories in *Refuge* are fiction, and not based on any person, living or dead, Fabia's work meant that I began this book having read the words of those who had made the voyage to Australia over the past two centuries. Fabia is a gem of a researcher — every question is answered with more richness and dedication than any writer could expect. The combined energies and determination of both Fabia and Noel Pratt were put to finding out exactly what Faris's situation would have been when he landed in Australia.

Once again Kate Burnitt has been the perfect editor, checking and rechecking details and consistency, incorporating correction after correction, each more illegible and with more crisscrossing arrows to spots in the text than the last.

And to the wonderful Kate O'Donnell too — enormous thanks for continuing to watch over the manuscripts.

It is difficult to convey how much Lisa Berryman of HarperCollins and Liz Kemp have added to and supported the creation of this work. The first draft that Lisa received was a vignette of a strange beach and a boy's journey. As they have so many times before, Lisa and Liz both urged and guided me into telling the full story, refusing to let the most important parts of the story — and the most difficult emotionally and intellectually to write — be left to the reader's imagination. (A row of dots is an all too easy cop-out.)

Without Lisa to say 'this doesn't work', I might never have attempted combining fantasy with so much realism. As with *Nanberry: Black Brother White* and *Pennies for Hitler*, *Refuge* is a far richer book for their guidance and friendship.

This book is about journeys. Its creation was a hard voyage as well. Many, many thanks to everyone whose inspiration and insight made it possible.

Titles by Jackie French

Australian Historical
Somewhere Around the Corner • Dancing with Ben Hall
Daughter of the Regiment • Soldier on the Hill • Valley of Gold
Tom Appleby, Convict Boy • A Rose for the Anzac Boys
The Night They Stormed Eureka • Nanberry: Black Brother White
Pennies for Hitler

General Historical
Hitler's Daughter • Lady Dance • How the Finnegans Saved the Ship
The White Ship • They Came on Viking Ships
Macbeth and Son • Pharaoh • Oracle
I am Juliet • Ophelia: Queen of Denmark
The Diary of William Shakespeare, Gentleman

Fiction
Rain Stones • Walking the Boundaries • The Secret Beach
Summerland • A Wombat Named Bosco • Beyond the Boundaries
The Warrior: The Story of a Wombat • The Book of Unicorns
Tajore Arkle • Missing You, Love Sara • Dark Wind Blowing
Ride the Wild Wind: The Golden Pony and Other Stories
Refuge • The Book of Horses and Unicorns

Non-Fiction
A Year in the Valley • How the Aliens from Alpha Centauri
Invaded My Maths Class and Turned Me into a Writer
How to Guzzle Your Garden • The Book of Challenges
The Fascinating History of Your Lunch
To the Moon and Back • The Secret World of Wombats
How High Can a Kangaroo Hop?
Let the Land Speak: How the Land Created Our Nation
I Spy a Great Reader

The Animal Stars Series
The Goat Who Sailed the World • The Dog Who Loved a Queen
The Camel Who Crossed Australia
The Donkey Who Carried the Wounded
The Horse Who Bit a Bushranger
Dingo: The Dog Who Conquered a Continent

The Matilda Saga
1. A Waltz for Matilda • 2. The Girl from Snowy River
3. The Road to Gundagai • 4. To Love a Sunburnt Country
5. The Ghost by the Billabong

The Secret Histories Series
Birrung the Secret Friend • Barney and the Secret of the Whales

Outlands Trilogy
In the Blood • Blood Moon • Flesh and Blood

School for Heroes Series
Lessons for a Werewolf Warrior • Dance of the Deadly Dinosaurs

Wacky Families Series
1. My Dog the Dinosaur • 2. My Mum the Pirate
3. My Dad the Dragon • 4. My Uncle Gus the Garden Gnome
5. My Uncle Wal the Werewolf • 6. My Gran the Gorilla
7. My Auntie Chook the Vampire Chicken • 8. My Pa the Polar Bear

Phredde Series
1. A Phaery Named Phredde
2. Phredde and a Frog Named Bruce
3. Phredde and the Zombie Librarian
4. Phredde and the Temple of Gloom
5. Phredde and the Leopard-Skin Librarian
6. Phredde and the Purple Pyramid
7. Phredde and the Vampire Footy Team
8. Phredde and the Ghostly Underpants

Picture Books
Diary of a Wombat (with Bruce Whatley)
Pete the Sheep (with Bruce Whatley)
Josephine Wants to Dance (with Bruce Whatley)
The Shaggy Gully Times (with Bruce Whatley)
Emily and the Big Bad Bunyip (with Bruce Whatley)
Baby Wombat's Week (with Bruce Whatley)
The Tomorrow Book (with Sue deGennaro)
Queen Victoria's Underpants (with Bruce Whatley)
Christmas Wombat (with Bruce Whatley)
A Day to Remember (with Mark Wilson)
Queen Victoria's Christmas (with Bruce Whatley)
Dinosaurs Love Cheese (with Nina Rycroft)
Wombat Goes to School (with Bruce Whatley)
The Hairy-Nosed Wombats Find a New Home (with Sue deGennaro)
Good Dog Hank (with Nina Rycroft)
The Beach They Called Gallipoli (with Bruce Whatley)
Wombat Wins (with Bruce Whatley)
Grandma Wombat (with Bruce Whatley)

Jackie French AM is an award-winning writer, wombat negotiator, the Australian Children's Laureate for 2014–2015 and the 2015 Senior Australian of the Year. She is regarded as one of Australia's most popular children's authors and writes across all genres — from picture books, history, fantasy, ecology and sci-fi to her much loved historical fiction. 'Share a Story' is the primary philosophy behind Jackie's two-year term as Laureate.

jackiefrench.com.au
facebook.com/authorjackiefrench